Ex-Texas Ranger's Attend **Finishing School**

"Refined Romance on the rugged frontier"

A Plus-Size Women's Frontier Romance Comedy

By Ms. Cherry Hargrove

Additional Books by author:

https://www.amazon.com/author/plussizewomensbooks

Table of Contents

I0642742

CHERRY HARGROVE

Main Characters

The Providence Ladies (The Mercy Six)

Graduates of Mercy College, Pennsylvania

Name	Personality	Calling
Ellie Whitcomb	Calm, wise, carries authority like quiet lightning	Leadership, administration, scripture
Naomi Brooks	Gentle spirit, prayer warrior	Spiritual guide, community peace
Maggie Ellis	Funny, joyful, flour-anointed baker	Bread ministry, food & fellowship
Ruth Ann Porter	Practical, observant, witty	Order, discipline, homemaking
Lillian Monroe	Sweet, refined, artistic	Etiquette, sewing, beauty & grace
Josie Carter	Warm, hospitable, slightly dramatic	Social graces, house welcome

The Six Rangers (The Reformed Rough Riders)

Name	Personality	Notes
Marshal Hayes	Confident, reformed wild-man	Leader, trying to be dignified
Benn Holt	Quiet, noble, deep thinker	Soft-spoken cowboy philosopher
Thomas Riley	Former preacher, dramatic	Quotes scripture... loudly
Boone Fletcher	Strong, stubborn, big-hearted	Etiquette enemy #1
Carter McGraw	Handsome, awkward, earnest	Romantic but clumsy
Hank Dawson	Sweet, young, easily flustered	Angel-hearted learner

Providence Town Map (Described)

Main Street

- General Store (Mrs. Brewer runs it)
- Barber & Baths
- Small church with white steeple
- Mayor's Hall
- Blacksmith & Livery
- Café that sells weak coffee but good gossip

Just off Main

- Mercy Ladies' Boardinghouse (top of little hill)
- Empty lots the ladies purchased (future bakery, school & sewing rooms)

Outskirts

- The Rangers' grand log lodge
- Pastures with cattle, horses, and pride

- Woods with prayer paths

Everything close enough to walk — and close enough for romance to observe.

CHAPTER ONE — THE STORM THAT DELIVERED US

The chapel at Mercy College gleamed in early summer light, every stained-glass pane shimmering as if the angels were leaning close to peer in. Six young women, bright-eyed and called by God, stood near the front pew, hands clasped, hearts steady even amid the excitement of graduation day. Ribbons graced their bonnets, gloves hugged their fingers, and hope, thick and sweet as sorghum, filled the air.

The organ hummed its final hymn as the dean spoke a blessing over them. He was a solemn, gentle man, with spectacles perched halfway down his nose and a voice that always seemed half-in prayer, even in conversation. He lifted his hands slowly, as if reluctant to send these bright daughters of the Lord into the unknown, but proud nonetheless.

"Ladies of Mercy College," he said, "go with grace, and go with purpose. The world does not always soften itself for women of calling, but heaven does not send calling where grace will not meet it. Be industrious, be courageous, and remember, the kingdom advances not only in pulpits and palaces, but in kitchens, schoolrooms, gardens, and quiet conversations where God whispers His plans."

Ellie Whitcomb's chin lifted, her expression calm, determined. She had a quiet command about her, the sort of presence that made people speak respectfully and children behave instinctively.

Naomi Brooks bowed her head gently, her voice a whisper only the Lord could hear. "Lead us, and we will follow."

Maggie Ellis sighed happily, clutching her hymnal like a promise. "And we will bake as we walk, Lord, because flour and faith do rise together."

Ruth Ann Porter, quick-witted but soft-voiced, pressed her lips into a line of reverence. Lillian Monroe tucked a loose curl under her bonnet with poise that spoke of finishing school discipline. Josie Carter smoothed her skirts and tried not to cry, though her eyes shone like morning dew.

Their classmates cheered softly, then embraced them. Lace sleeves brushed lace sleeves, gloved hands squeezed, tears fell but only the joyful kind—the kind that felt like stepping into destiny.

Outside, the train whistle called, long and sure, like the Lord's own trumpet saying, "It is time."

The six women boarded with traveling trunks and tidy prayer journals, their pin money safely hidden in their bodices—four hundred dollars each, earned through sewing lessons, baking commissions, scripture-copying contracts, scholarship awards, and a remarkable frugality known only to determined women of virtue with large dreams. It was not wealth, not in the world's measure, but it was faith sewn into coin, and faith multiplies.

The countryside rolled by—green pastures, low hills, small farms with chickens scattering near fences, cows grazing lazily, wildflowers nodding like ladies at a summer garden party. The ladies spoke in quiet tones of their plans.

"Our school shall be a place of refinement and scripture," Ellie said, hands folded primly.

"And baking," Maggie added quickly. "And bread business lessons, and how to run a proper community kitchen. And perhaps a pie society. The Lord does love cheerful bakers."

Naomi laughed softly. "In fairness, He loves cheerful anyone."

Josie tucked a stray thread into her glove. "Do you suppose we shall have many students?"

"We shall have exactly whom the Lord sends," Ruth Ann replied calmly. "And He wastes no assignments."

Lillian, always the one to dream big and speak softly, whispered, "Perhaps we shall build not only a school, but a bakery, and a modest dressmaking shop, and a place for girls to learn hospitality and confidence. A place where plus-size women"— she raised her chin here, proud and unashamed— "are cherished and taught their worth."

The others murmured "amen" like birdsong.

Hours passed sweetly, filled with hymns hummed under breath, sandwiches eaten from wax paper, and windows watched with anticipation. Then, near late afternoon, the sky shifted. Clouds gathered thick and quick, as though the heavens suddenly remembered a storm they had meant to pour earlier.

The wind picked up, rattling the train car slightly. Ellie frowned at the sky. Naomi lifted a hand to her chest.

"Ladies," Ellie murmured, "brace yourselves."

The conductor strode down the aisle. "Storm's coming in swift, folks. Hold steady. We'll outrun most of it, but she might nip our heels."

He hadn't finished his sentence when the wind howled like a fiddle string snapping. Rain slapped the windows sideways. The train jolted. Ladies gasped. A few men shouted. Children cried.

But the Mercy College six?

Their hair lifted from their heads as if heaven itself tugged it upward. Maggie's ribbon stood straight like a banner. Lillian's curls billowed. Josie's hat nearly took flight until Ruth Ann snatched it mid-air. Naomi's shawl fluttered like angel wings. Ellie's bonnet strings whipped in a dramatic fashion that would have frightened a lesser woman, but she gripped the seat and smiled faintly.

A shrill whistle of wind filled the cabin, and the train slowed under its force. Steam hissed. A cow outside flew past so fast that Josie blinked twice, unsure if she had seen a cow or a blessing disguised as livestock.

But instead of screaming, instead of panic, instead of despair, the young women began praising.

Naomi lifted her face toward the rattling roof. "Lord, You guided Noah. You guided Moses. Guide this locomotive and our mission."

Ruth Ann grinned through wind-tousled hair. "We are still in the palm of Your hand."

Lillian clapped a hand to her bonnet. "And if we must fly, Lord, please land us standing upright."

Maggie burst into laughter so joyous it startled half the passengers. "Ladies, we look like revival tent meetings on wash day!"

Even Ellie, calm as psalms written in sunlight, gave a small chuckle. "We shall not be undone by wind. The breath of God only sends us where we must go."

Then, after what felt like an eternity and a hymn stanza or two sung silently, the storm eased. Rain softened to a sprinkle; the rattling slowed; the train exhaled steam like a grateful ox after a long pull.

Passengers looked stunned. A few applauded. Someone whispered, "Those women prayed us through."

And perhaps they had.

The train rolled forward again, slower now, cautious. It wasn't long before it came to an unexpected stop at a station not on their itinerary.

The sign read:

PROVIDENCE, MISSOURI

Where God Provides

"What town is this?" Josie asked.

"God's hint," Naomi murmured.

The conductor appeared. "Ladies, this is a temporary stop for repairs. Might be a spell. You're welcome to stretch your legs."

Stretch they did and embarked off the train.

Providence was small—wooden storefronts, a church with a white steeple, a general store with barrels out front, a modest restaurant, the sheriff's office, hitching posts, and a scattering of curious faces peering from porches and windows.

Two men approached—one broad-shouldered in a sheriff's badge and biblical confidence, the other in a mayor's sash and civic pride.

"Ladies," the sheriff said, tipping his hat. "Welcome to Providence. Heard your train tangled with the good Lord's wind."

Ellie nodded. "Only delivered us where we are meant to be."

The mayor blinked, impressed. "Spoken like someone who knows divine appointments."

Naomi smiled. "We go where He directs. We intended Kansas, but God intends obedience, not geography."

Maggie sniffed the air. "And I smell opportunity... and pie cooling somewhere nearby."

The mayor chuckled. "You bake?"

Maggie placed a hand over her heart. "Sir, I do not bake. I minister with flour."

Ruth Ann whispered, "She speaks truth."

The sheriff cleared his throat. "Miss, if you intend to stay—"

"We do," Ellie said simply.

Their certainty startled even themselves. They had not planned to say it. But the Holy Spirit sometimes answers questions before lips do.

Josie leaned close to Ellie. "Did... did we just move?"

"Yes," Ellie whispered. "Apparently we have."

The mayor brightened. "Well then, Providence welcomes you. We have need of teachers, bakers, seamstresses, scripture-minded women. And, if I may say it plain, our town has at least six good men who have prayed for wives."

The ladies exchanged startled glances. Maggie coughed. Naomi hid a smile. Josie blushed. Ellie did not blink.

"We have prayed for purpose," Ellie said calmly. "The Lord shall arrange the rest."

Within hours, they were shown an old boardinghouse—a grand thing once, with wrap-around porch, high ceilings, creaking floors, and dusty lace curtains. The roof sagged slightly, the wallpaper peeled, the kitchen needed scrubbing and a soul, but oh, the potential.

"This could be our home," Lillian whispered, touching a carved banister, eyes shimmering.

"And our school," Naomi added.

"And our bakery," Maggie breathed reverently.

Josie pressed both hands to her mouth. "We could host teas. Bible lessons. Sewing circles."

Ruth Ann lifted her chin. "Ladies, shall we?"

They didn't debate. They nodded as one, like prayer partners agreeing with heaven.

Later that afternoon, at the lawyer's office, they signed the deed —six names, six futures, one calling. Their partial pin money covered it, with enough left for food, supplies, and a few new ribbons.

That night, they slept on mattresses borrowed from the hotel, quilts wrapped around them, yet sleep did not come from down feathers but from the deep satisfaction of obedience.

Outside, the townsfolk whispered at porches.

"Six new ladies, all fine and educated."

"Surely wives for someone."

"They're too industrious to stay unclaimed long."

Out on the ridge, six ex-Texas Rangers sat by lamplight at their large homestead lodge—rough, loyal men who had carved a life in wilderness and prayed, in stumbling masculine fashion, for God to someday send them wives who were not frightened by calloused hands and big dreams.

Marshal Hayes squinted toward town. "Heard some ladies arrived."

Carter McGraw scratched his chin. "Heard they're proper. Schooling folks."

Boone Fletcher grunted. "Hope they ain't the bossy sort."

Thomas Riley, former circuit preacher, narrowed his eyes gently. "I prayed for a woman who knows scripture. Gentle but strong."

Benn Holt murmured, "And soft-hearted."

Hank Dawson whispered, "And kind to a man tryin' to be better."

They did not know it yet, but heaven had already said yes.

In the boardinghouse, Ellie whispered a final prayer before sleep. "Lord, guide our steps."

On the ranch porch, Marshal whispered, "Lord, guide our wives to us."

And the Lord, who delights in holy humor, whispered back into both night skies, "Patience, children. Refinement first."

The wind rustled leaves like a soft hymn.

Destiny settled into place.

And Providence, Missouri slept with expectation on its breath.

CHAPTER TWO — SETTLING PROVIDENCE AND STIRRING CURIOSITY

Morning broke softly over Providence, Missouri, the sky washed in pink like the inside of a seashell. Birdsong fluttered at the windows of the newly acquired boardinghouse, and sunlight tiptoed across floors waiting for polish and purpose. Six women rose from borrowed quilts with stiff backs, but joyful hearts, stretching like lilies waking in spring. Destiny might come on wings, but it also woke up in modest rooms with dust motes dancing in sunbeams and a kettle waiting to be boiled.

Ellie hummed as she pinned her hair, smoothing any strands the storm had mischievously rearranged the evening before. Naomi folded quilts carefully. Josie fussed over lace trim she insisted must be crisp. Ruth Ann wiped down a washbasin, sniffing once at the lingering dust but tackling it like a soldier of sanitation. Maggie started water for coffee, which she considered essential to revival and order. Lillian took stock of the few utensils they possessed.

No one complained. Faith, when rooted deep, produces gratitude even when the floor creaks, paint flakes, and windows sigh from long-ignored hinges.

Maggie stirred the pot. "Imagine it, ladies. Soon this kitchen shall shine. There will be bread rising on all counters, pies cooling on windowsills, and biscuits so fluffy heaven will pause to admire them."

Naomi laughed lightly. "Let the Lord admire our prayers first, Maggie, then our biscuits."

"He often does both," Maggie replied, tapping the spoon against the pot with reverence. "Our God appreciates a good loaf."

Josie tightened her bonnet ribbon. "There is an order to all refinement: prayer, planning, polite society, and then pastries."

"Is that in Scripture?" Ruth Ann teased.

"It should be," Josie answered solemnly.

They bowed their heads in the little front parlor, where no proper pew existed but reverence did. Ellie prayed with calm certainty.

"Lord, thank You for safe arrival. We dedicate this house to Your glory. Make it a haven for learning, for feeding hearts and minds, for raising up women and—if You choose—godly homes one day. Grant us patience, humor, and diligence. Where the boards creak, lay Your peace. Where paint flakes, lay Your purpose. And when men come knocking, let discernment answer the door first."

They chorused, "Amen."

As if heaven wanted to respond with gentle laughter, a rooster crowed loudly from the yard.

Lillian peeked through the curtain. "We have neighbors."

Naomi joined her. "And apparently livestock. That rooster seems earnest."

Maggie lifted her eyebrows. "The Lord gives us a loud welcome sometimes."

Within the hour, they set off toward town to purchase cleaning supplies and speak with the lawyer again about land rights. They walked gracefully, skirts swaying, parasols lifted lightly, their presence drawing as many stares as sparrows draw when they land in a quiet field suddenly turned lively.

Providence was not a large town, but it was a hopeful one. Men hammering boards looked up and nearly hammered their thumbs. A farmer selling greens paused mid-shout. Merchants leaned out of doorways. Young boys froze mid-marble game. Even older women, seasoned by life and mothering and church committees, slowed visibly to take in the sight of six refined ladies walking like purpose was stitched into their hems.

Maggie whispered, "We seem to be causing stir."

Ruth Ann murmured back, "Like fresh honey at a bee meeting."

Inside the lawyer's office, papers were reviewed once more. Land here was inexpensive, and, as Naomi put it, "God wastes nothing, not even acreage." They purchased an additional one acre each in town—future sites for their ventures. The lawyer blinked as though uncertain if Providence had suddenly become the capital of women's ownership.

"You ladies understand," he said with awkward gravity, "this much land, plus a boardinghouse, means... independence."

"Yes," Ellie replied pleasantly. "We are aware."

He swallowed. "And you intend to... run businesses?"

Naomi smiled. "In a godly manner, sir."

He nodded, slightly intimidated, then signed the papers.

As they left, two store clerks across the street nearly collided trying to hold the door open for them, whispering loud enough to be heard.

"Which one you think'll wed first?"

"Hush! They ain't here for that... probably."

Maggie whispered, "Bless their hearts."

At the general store, they purchased flour, soap, fabric, ribbons, and sturdy work aprons. The shopkeeper, a respectable older widow named Mrs. Brewer, watched them with wisdom gleaming.

"You're the new Mercy ladies," she said. "The town's speaking blessing and curiosity both. You plan to teach?"

Ellie nodded. "And bake. Sew. Build community."

Mrs. Brewer leaned in conspiratorially. "And you will be courted, make no mistake. Our menfolk have prayed droughts away with less determination."

Naomi's cheeks pinked softly. "We have prayed for purpose first."

"Purpose draws partners when God approves," Mrs. Brewer replied knowingly. "And He just might be stirring pots already."

The women concluded their purchases and left with gratitude, prayer, and slightly amused apprehension.

By midday, they returned to the boardinghouse to begin cleaning. Window sashes rattled. Dust flew like startled birds. Rugs were beaten on the porch, sending clouds into the yard. Naomi scrubbed baseboards with scripture in her breath. Ellie mopped with dignity befitting a queen. Lillian polished brass with notable precision. Josie washed windows until they gleamed. Maggie churned biscuits between tasks, for nourishment was ministry, and Ruth Ann oversaw the placement of furniture with architectural authority.

When the smell of biscuits drifted across the yard, Providence noticed. That aroma carried promise, possibility, and perhaps pie-shaped prophecy.

By late afternoon, footsteps approached. Neighbors brought small gifts—flour sacks, a quilt square, a jar of honey. One young man brought apples and blushed so fiercely Ruth Ann nearly blessed him with cold water for relief.

Then came the mayor.

He removed his hat respectfully. "Ladies, good day. Providence is well pleased to have you."

Ellie nodded with grace. "We are honored to serve the community."

The mayor shifted. "I do come with a suggestion. Opportunity, one might say."

Ruth Ann's eyebrow lifted. "We are listening."

He cleared his throat. "A group of ex-Texas Rangers resides just outside town. Six of them. Hard-working men, God-fearing, though in need of gentle refinement. They have prayed for wives, specifically plus-size, modest, soft-spoken, nurturing sort."

Naomi pressed lips to stifle a smile. "Specific petitioners."

"Yes," the mayor admitted. "They believe in a... certain wife ideal."

Maggie smirked. "They shall be educated."

He nodded earnestly. "They hope to court through mail-order bride efforts, but truthfully, they need instruction first. How to speak politely. Dress properly. Behave in mixed company. A touch of civility, you understand."

Josie folded her hands. "And you propose?"

"That they pay you five dollars per month each and assist in repairs here, in exchange for... etiquette education."

Silence lingered, thick with divine humor.

Ruth Ann asked, "Refinement lessons for unrefined men?"

"Precisely."

Ellie exchanged looks with the others. The prayer in her eyes was not for romance, but assignment. "We will pray on it. Return this evening, Mayor."

He tipped hat. "Ladies."

When he left, Maggie whirled. "Do you realize? They think we are mail-order preparers, not ministry builders."

Josie giggled. "Imagine men believing they control destiny while women refine it."

Naomi straightened. "We do not accept lightly. We pray."

And they did.

Six women knelt on hardwood planks, skirts fanned like petals around them, and each lifted her voice.

"Lord, if this is Your assignment, give us peace."

"If this is distraction, close the door."

"If these men seek wives without wisdom, give us grace to teach."

"If Your hand guides, let us know."

Lillian spoke last. "And if they think docility means lack of purpose, we shall show them Proverbs 31 in action."

The Spirit settled peace like a soft quilt over them.

"We will do it," Ellie whispered.

Evening fell, lanterns glowed, supper was simple soup and biscuits, and joy filled cracks where dust once settled. When the mayor returned, they gave their answer.

"We will teach," Ellie said, "after church each Sunday, four hours, for six months. In exchange, the men will repair this house thoroughly, bring one delivery of provisions each Friday, and attend service washed, groomed, shaven, and in clean attire. They shall sit respectfully and quietly in worship. They shall practice Christian hospitality. They shall demonstrate humility."

The mayor blinked, awe dawning. "You ladies do not go halfway."

"We are not half-called," Naomi replied gently.

And thus, an arrangement was struck. A holy, humorous contract heaven likely applauded.

Early next morning, a young ranch hand approached, shy but respectful, dusted apron-clean as if trying to impress the angels themselves. He introduced himself as Hank, though the ranch leader had not yet appeared.

"I come on behalf of the fellas," he said, removing his hat. "Food delivery Friday. They're mighty nervous. They've never done lessons. They tried to iron shirts and almost burned the ranch."

Maggie gasped. "Ironing mishaps are a trial of character."

"Yes, ma'am. They're prayin' heavily."

Ellie smiled. "Tell them we pray also."

He bobbed his head, cheeks warm. "Yes, ma'am. Also... they heard rumors men in town have taken interest. They say thank you kindly for keepin' competition fair."

Ruth Ann's eyes sparkled. "Providence has no shortage of eager hearts."

Hank nodded gravely. "That scares them real bad."

"They need not fear," Ellie assured him. "God appoints all futures."

Hank sighed in relief as though someone freed his soul. "Thank the Lord."

By the time Friday arrived, Providence men were circling the boardinghouse like bees near spring blossoms. Every eligible bachelor in a fifty-mile radius seemed suddenly fond of walking past the gate, adjusting hat, offering to carry water, or claiming need to inspect the siding for weather damage.

But etiquette, like divine timing, does not rush. The women greeted every gentleman courteously, praised every effort, yet returned to duty quickly, allowing curiosity to simmer without boiling.

Town gossip grew warm.

"They're fixin' to marry, mark me."
"No, they're building first."
"Building? You mean a future?"
"And bakery."
"And school."
"And possibly a pie ministry."

On Sunday, when church bells rang, neighbors tidied collars, ladies chose bonnets twice as carefully, and whispers trailed across pews like hymn-soft wind.

But the six women walked in calm, prayerful dignity, lace gloves folded and only God seen.

Behind them, six ex-Rangers had entered the sanctuary, faces serious, boots shined so hard they might blind, hair combed into submission, and souls trembling like lambs before an altar of refinement.

The pastor nearly dropped his Bible.

The congregation held its breath.

Women glanced subtly; young men frowned with envy; older matrons nodded in solemn approval.

And when worship began, reverence swelled.

By service's end, every heart in Providence knew a divine story had begun — one that braided duty, destiny, romance, and prayer like a perfect loaf rising.

After church, the women departed for the boardinghouse, their parasols elegant shields. The Rangers followed humbly, then a crowd of bachelors, eager like spring calves, attempted to follow also.

Josie politely halted them at the porch. "Class is full. Next term in six months."

A groan rolled through town like thunder.

Inside, chairs were set, tea ready, biscuits warm, napkins crisp, and grace waited.

Refinement had begun.

And heaven, with holy humor, smiled.

CHAPTER THREE — REFINEMENT BEGINS WITH PIE AND PRAYER

Sunday afternoon arrived with sunlight soft as silk and a hush across Providence that felt like expectation and curiosity braided together. The church bell had barely finished its final chime when the six Mercy College women returned to the boardinghouse. Their steps were graceful, their expressions composed, yet inside their hearts fluttered like doves ready to take flight.

After church, they entered the kitchen not with flurry, but with purpose; their movements smooth, their teamwork precise, like a symphony tuning before glory. Flour dust danced in sun beams; butter softened in bowls; spices perfumed the air. Tea leaves waited like jewels beside a polished kettle.

Ellie arranged the china, setting each delicate cup as if preparing a royal table. Naomi arranged napkins and silverware with precise grace, murmuring a psalm under her breath. Maggie shaped biscuits and checked pies, her lips moving in quiet praise, as if baking itself was prayer. Lillian added ribbon to fresh floral sprigs and placed them in jars on the table. Ruth Ann stirred gravy, stirring also gentle dignity into each motion. Josie dusted the final cinnamon over apple slices, smiling as though she already saw the Lord's blessing upon every dish.

The dining room, though still modest, shone with care: lace cleaned and pressed, chairs positioned, cutlery aligned, sunlight filtering across polished wood like heaven acknowledging labor done unto the Lord.

Their clothing had been pressed again, bonnets fluffed, gloves smoothed. They did not dress to impress men; they dressed as if presenting themselves to purpose.

A soft knock sounded at the door.

Lillian peeked from the kitchen. "They are here."

The Rangers stood awkwardly on the porch, hats in hand, hair slicked into submission, boots polished, suits strained in seams. They looked like warriors who had attempted to transform into gentlemen overnight and were uncertain if the transformation had taken full effect.

Ellie opened the door with calm dignity. "Good afternoon, gentlemen. Please come in."

Marshal Hayes stepped in first, breathing carefully as though the air inside the boardinghouse was higher quality than he was accustomed to. Boone tried to bow but came dangerously close to head-butting the doorframe. Carter held his hat as though afraid it would misbehave. Hank entered as reverently as a man stepping into church. Benn nodded politely, brim of his hat trembling from nerves. Thomas held his prayer book like a shield.

The men sat very straight, perched precariously on chairs as though they expected correction for breathing incorrectly.

Ellie addressed them warmly. "Welcome to your first lesson. We begin with grace."

All heads bowed. Naomi prayed soft yet strong:

Lord, refine us all. Grow humility in hearts, patience in spirits, discipline in tongues, and gentleness in hands. May pride fall like dust beneath holy rain, and may we feast on grace more than biscuits. Amen.

"Amen," the men echoed, some with trembling sincerity.

Then came the instruction.

Josie lifted a teacup. "You will practice handling china as if it were newborn lambs."

Boone blinked. "We can hold lambs."

"Not the same," Ruth Ann murmured.

Lillian set the first plate gently. "Gentlemen, posture upright. Shoulders relaxed. Forks held delicately. Napkins in laps."

Hank placed his napkin so carefully it could have been a Bible.

Carter sat still as a schoolchild on inspection day.

Boone whispered, "I don't know what to do with my elbows."

"Down," all six women replied in unison.

Marshal attempted a dignified pose, but his left boot squeaked loudly against the chair rung. He flinched like he had committed treason.

Thomas inhaled deeply. "Lord give me poise."

Naomi nodded approvingly. "He shall."

Then came food.

Maggie brought out biscuits steaming with butter, and men's eyes widened like they beheld manna. Ruth Ann followed with roasted chicken and dressing, Lillian with honey-glazed carrots, Ellie with golden bread, Josie with fresh jam, Naomi with gravy rich enough to redeem a weary soul.

The men sat frozen, half afraid to inhale too fast lest they disgrace themselves in the presence of such culinary anointing.

Ellie gestured gently. "You may serve yourselves."

Boone tried to pass the biscuits but nearly flung one before catching it mid-air. Naomi steadied his hand. "Slow, Mr. Fletcher."

"Yes ma'am."

Carter cut chicken as though learning surgery. Hank whispered scripture for strength. Benn sweated from effort alone. Marshal mumbled, "For the Lord and refinement." Thomas prayed between bites whether he meant to or not.

Then they tasted.

Marshal Hayes nearly melted. "This... this must be heavenly issued."

Boone took a bite of biscuit and shut his eyes reverently. "Saints never ate better, I'm convinced."

Hank dabbed his napkin so carefully it was almost angelic. "Miss Maggie, ma'am, this biscuit... it speaks."

Maggie's eyes softened. "It says grace rises when dough rests."

Boone took another bite. "It also says 'eat more.'"

The ladies suppressed smiles.

Thomas lifted pie to his mouth and whispered, "I repent for every flavorless meal I've ever accepted."

Carter sighed into his tea. "If refinement tastes like this, maybe God loves us more than I knew."

And then came etiquette.

Josie reminded, "No gulping."

Naomi instructed, "No talking with food in mouth."

Ruth Ann, helpful but firm, tapped Boone's wrist. "Slow chewing."

Ellie added scripture, "Let all things be done decently and in order."

Marshal whispered to Boone, "Decent chewing saved me today."

Boone whispered back, "Decent chewing nearly killed me, from slowness."

Dessert arrived. Silence fell again.

Every man stared. Six slices of pie rested like sacramental offerings.

Hank whispered, "Lord, I am not worthy."

Josie nodded. "Eat anyway."

Benn's fork trembled. Boone exhaled awe. Thomas sniffed pie as though confirming holiness. Carter stared in adoration. Marshal closed his eyes like tasting revelation.

After the last crumb vanished, napkins were folded, chairs pushed back carefully, and six men sat breathing as though they had run a mile uphill carrying righteousness on their backs.

Ellie stood. "Next week we practice polite conversation and posture."

Boone grimaced in fear. "More posture?"

Naomi nodded. "Refinement is not a sprint. It is sanctification."

Thomas whispered, "Lord, give us endurance."

And with that, the men rose—slowly, stiffly, reverently. Hats in hand. Souls slightly altered. Bellies full enough to shift gravity.

Marshal cleared his throat. "Ma'ams… we thank you."

Benn added, "We are learning."

Boone mumbled, "And suffering."

Carter wheezed, "From biscuits."

Hank whispered, "I believe in sanctification through pie."

Thomas nodded solemnly. "We shall return humbled."

Josie smiled sweetly. "We expect it."

The men staggered to the porch. It was a dignified stagger, but a stagger nonetheless. Their belts felt tighter. Their souls felt heavier with conviction. Their bodies felt bowed beneath the weight of gravy and grace.

Outside, sunlight glowed. Their horses waited.

Boone stared at his horse and whispered, "I don't think I can mount today."

Marshal rubbed his stomach. "My bones feel buttered."

Hank leaned forward with effort. "I thought refinement meant posture, not digestion warfare."

Carter clutched his middle. "I'm fairly certain pie has weight of glory."

Thomas adjusted his vest like oxygen was optional. "This must be how saints feel after banquet halls in glory."

Benn groaned softly. "If sanctification requires eating like this weekly, I fear for my horse."

Boone nodded fervently. "We should have asked to take leftovers home. We could have survived on them three days."

Marshal shook his head. "We must not appear greedy."

Boone glared. "Greed isn't the sin today. Explosion is."

Hank swallowed gingerly. "Brothers, I cannot lift myself onto that saddle without divine intervention."

Thomas placed a hand on his shoulder. "Then pray, Hank. For the spirit is willing, but the flesh is... heavy."

They prayed again, not for salvation this time, but for digestion and strength to hoist themselves into saddles without collapsing or dishonoring the Lord's good biscuits.

Eventually, with much grunting, one whispered psalm, several near-miss falls, and one loud "Lord have mercy!" they mounted and rode.

Not galloping. Not trotting.

A slow, painful, solemn plod.

Like men gentle-broken by biscuits, gravy, and holy feminine refinement.

On the ridge, half-way home, Marshal sighed. "Five more months and three weeks."

Boone groaned. "We won't survive."

Carter whispered, "If we perish, bury me with pie crumbs."

Thomas breathed heavily. "We must not faint. We are men of faith."

Hank clutched his side. "Faith hurts."

Benn looked heavenward. "Lord, strengthen our backs and our stomachs. And next time, help us take home leftovers."

And the horses, bless their patient souls, carried them onward, heads bobbing gently as if amused by the sight of refined warriors in pastry pain.

Back at the boardinghouse, six women watched from the curtain, smiling faintly, then bowed their heads again in gratitude and silent laughter.

Maggie whispered, "Lord, bless those men. They will need Your help next week."

Naomi nodded. "We all will."

Ellie closed the drape, heart steady. "And we shall give it."

Providence slept that night under the hands of God, while six men lay flat on their backs whispering vows to pace themselves, and six women dreamed of schools, bakeries, dignity, and the gentle hand of grace working slowly on rugged hearts.

The first week had begun.

Refinement and romance—both still young sprouts—had taken root.

And heaven, amused and pleased, smiled again.

CHAPTER FOUR — "GENTLEMEN IN PRACTICE, SAINTS IN PROGRESS"

The next morning dawned bright, as if heaven itself wanted to inspect the Mercy Six's progress.

Birds chirped. Biscuits rose. And Maggie hummed like warm honey spreading on toast.

Josie peeked out the window and whispered, "Ladies... Boone is practicing walking slow in front of the boardinghouse."

Maggie nearly choked laughing. "Bless him, Lord, he's walking like his spine forgot what its job is."

Naomi placed a hand over her mouth. "He looks like he's carrying invisible fragile china."

Ellie lifted her brow approvingly. "At least improvement is attempting itself."

Ruth Ann watched Boone stiff-leg shuffle past again, jaw clenched in masculine suffering.

"He is walking like someone told him pride was a coat and he put it on backwards."

The ladies laughed softly.

Scripture floated through the room as Naomi read, "Let patience have her perfect work."

James 1:4

"Amen," they said, sipping tea like queens with broom handles waiting.

Just then — WHAP.

They all jumped. Lillian gasped. "What was that?"

Josie peeked out again. "Thomas Riley just fell attempting to bow to Mrs. Brewer."

Maggie clasped her chest. "Oh bless him, Lord. Refinement is trying to kill them before it saves them."

Naomi murmured sweetly, "We shall bury them with biscuits if needed."

Lillian whispered, dramatic, "He fell in holiness."

"I dare say," Ellie replied, "he fell in confusion."

A soft knock sounded. Ellie opened the door to find the sheriff holding a jar of peaches.

"Mornin', ladies," he said gently. "The boys asked me to deliver this. They are... emotionally winded from practicing."

"Emotionally winded," Ruth Ann repeated. "Is that new or inherited?"

Sheriff Porter coughed to hide a smile. "They also requested— very humbly— tomorrow's meal portion be modest. Carter said if he eats that much holiness again, he may ascend early."

Maggie nodded solemnly. "Heaven forbid."

"And Marshal says," the sheriff added, "he's been rehearin' thank-you phrases so much he complimented a fence post."

Ellie accepted the peaches. "Tell them we are praying for their strength."

"And their chairs," Maggie added.

Sheriff tipped his hat. "And ladies... there may be... murmurs at church today."

Naomi smiled sweetly. "Murmurs? Providence needs murmurs for seasoning. We shall bring grace."

He left shaking his head, muttering, "Lord, protect them men."

The ladies stood a moment in holy silence.

Then Josie straightened her ribbon. "Let us go to church."

"And be gracious," Ellie added.

"And not faint over them in their new collars," Maggie teased.

"God forbid," Naomi blushed.

They stepped outside as six Rangers approached in tidy rows — starched, solemn, stomachs still hurting.

Marshal bowed and nearly pulled a muscle.

"Ladies."

"Good morning," Ellie said, regal as psalm.

Boone whispered to Carter, "Do not... over compliment... or bow aggressively."

Thomas held his Bible trembling. "If the Lord wanted humility, He should've given me weaker pride."

Naomi whispered a sweet prayer over them. "Lord bless these men, for they know not the trials of etiquette."

As they walked toward church together, shoulders aligned, steps aligned, **destiny aligned**.

Maggie whispered to Ellie, "Do you realize... the Lord is matchmaking with manners?"

Ellie smiled softly. "He works in mysterious biscuits."

The week passed like honey poured warm from heaven — slow, sweet, and wonderfully sticky. Every morning, the Mercy Six woke with light hearts and sore ribs from laughing about the Rangers' first etiquette lesson. Never had refinement been such a holy comedy.

At breakfast, someone inevitably started the retelling.

Maggie would sigh dramatically, "Ladies, Boone Fletcher bowed like a windmill losing power. I thought his legs were going to fall right off his dignity."

Josie nearly spilled her tea. "And Marshal Hayes prayed over the gravy like it was battle strategy!"

Lillian dabbed her eyes daily. "Thomas Riley attacked that pie as if it contained every message from the Book of Revelation."

Naomi, ever gentle, shook her head. "Bless them. They tried. And they nearly fainted under the weight of butter and hope."

Ellie's eyes sparkled despite her composed expression. "We must remember, ladies — they gave their whole hearts. And nearly their belts."

By Wednesday the story had grown enough details to fill a stage play, and each time it came alive in the kitchen again, someone had to stop to catch their breath before laughter made them faint. There are seasons when joy is worship, and Providence was in one.

Yet work did not stop. The boardinghouse hummed with feminine industry and purpose — sweeping, scrubbing, sewing, baking, praying, selling baked goods and mended clothes to townsfolk who, bless them, found any excuse to visit.

The place became a hive. No honeybees in sight, yet sweet buzz everywhere.

Tuesday brought a line of bachelors with handkerchiefs and hopes, trying to purchase biscuits and inquire — ever so innocently — about "the next class signup list."

"Six months," Ellie reminded one hopeful young barber.

"Six months?" he gasped like someone learning winter lasted until July. "Lord give me strength."

"Pray also for patience," Naomi added kindly.

"I shall," he whispered, hand over heart.

By Thursday the town was whispering louder than church ladies after revival service.

"They came to build businesses, not marry—so they say."
"Well, hearts have a habit of building their own plans."
"Those ex-Rangers look cleaner each Sunday… almost alarming."

Meanwhile, the Rangers spent their days out in the pastures, grateful for hard labor that reminded them who they were before napkins and tiny forks changed their worldview.

Boone swung a hay fork with vigor. "If I see fine china again this week, somebody read Psalms over me."

Marshal rubbed his stomach gently. "I've had battlefield wounds hurt less than refined eating."

Hank leaned on a fence post, staring into the horizon. "Do you reckon etiquette can cause spiritual soreness?"

Thomas looked heavenward. "Sanctification isn't painless. I believe we are being kneaded like bread dough."

Benn nodded solemnly. "They softened my pride like butter."

Carter muttered, "That pie softened everything."

And then they sighed — long, thoughtful, stomach-war torn sighs.

But each evening, without fail, they cleaned themselves up, combed hair, practiced posture in the lodge hallway, and tried to remember which fork was designed for which glory.

"We can make it six months," Marshal declared.

Hank whispered, "Lord, that's a millennium in pie years."

Friday arrived bright and fair, with the smell of anticipation in the wind and flour in the boardinghouse air.

Hank rode up with a wagon piled comically high — sacks of flour, sugar, honey, potatoes, jars of peaches, fresh butter, a whole sack of coffee beans, and a small crate decorated with a bow that screamed Boone Fletcher had attempted domestic contribution.

Maggie came to the porch wiping her hands. "Mercy. Y'all feeding a church revival?"

Hank swallowed nervously. "The fellas... uh... said last week you fed us like saints in the Promised Land. They want you to have all the supplies necessary to do the Lord's work."

Ruth Ann opened the crate and stared. "Is this... cinnamon?"

"Yes ma'am," Hank said proudly. "We didn't know how much

goes in fancy cookin', so we got six pounds."

Lillian blinked. "Six pounds? For refinement or resurrection?"

Naomi lifted the lid of another box. "Is this china again?"

"Tea saucers," Hank whispered reverently. "Boone says y'all might host tea for angels."

Josie laughed so hard she had to lean against the doorframe. "Bless that man. Tea for angels."

Hank shifted nervously. "He says we must impress heaven before we court earth."

Ellie smiled softly. "Good theology for a courting man."

Hank blushed. "We ain't courting. We're learning. That's what Marshal keeps sayin' anyway."

"And you believe him?" Ruth Ann teased.

Hank opened and closed his mouth like a fish tossed ashore. "Ma'am... I am simply afflicted with obedience."

They carried the goods in, stacked them in the pantry, and whispered thanks to God for provision. Providence did not lack its name.

All week, the ladies had worked on sewing new dresses — fine ones, with clean seams, lace trim, and satin ribbon at waists — Sunday best for lessons that felt like stepping into calling. But every time they attempted to finish a hem, a knock sounded on the door. Someone needed a biscuit order. Someone needed scripture printed. Someone hoped to sniff the air and catch a vision of refinement.

These women could not finish a sleeve without answering a question, directing supplies, assigning a chore suggestion, or kindly redirecting a bachelor who nearly pitched himself into service out of sheer hopefulness.

By Friday evening, dresses sat half-finished.

Ruth Ann tied her measuring string in a knot and sighed. "We have eight sleeves and only three correct armholes."

Naomi patted her shoulder. "The Lord asks obedience, not

perfection."

Lillian held up a bodice. "This one got sewn wrong-side out. Twice."

Maggie waved a spoon like a sword. "It's fine. We will distract them with biscuits and they won't notice threads."

Josie giggled. "They are too busy trying to survive napkin use. We are safe."

Ellie nodded. "We serve God. Seamstresses second."

The week passed in prayer, pies, and preparation. On Saturday afternoon they arranged cut flowers in jars, swept the parlor, polished china again, and prayed over the front door.

Naomi recited, "Let your gentleness be known unto all men. The Lord is at hand."

Philippians 4:5

"Amen," everyone whispered.

Sunday morning

Church bells rang like silver announcements. Hats sat perfect, bonnets tied neatly, gloves buttoned, hair smoothed — though Maggie claimed humidity was the devil's hairstylist.

The Rangers arrived unexpectedly early, as if afraid tardiness would revoke their salvation and pie privileges. They stood straighter than fence posts, boots shined, hair combed shiny, shirts ironed so crisp Marshal flinched each time he bent an elbow.

Josie whispered behind her hymnal, "Look at them. Like gospel soldiers."

Maggie smiled. "Bless their hearts. And their stomachs."

Ellie nodded respectfully to the men as they approached. "Good morning, gentlemen."

Marshal bowed with caution. "Ladies."

Boone said nothing — he was concentrating on breathing quietly.

Carter attempted a compliment. "You look... well-appointed for the Lord."

Maggie's eyes twinkled. "And you look appointed for mercy."

Naomi leaned toward Ruth Ann. "We must not laugh. It is cruel."

Ruth Ann replied, "Cruel? Perhaps. Impossible? Certainly."

Church began. The men sat rigid, elbows glued to ribs, heads bowed in reverence mixed with fear of etiquette failure. When hymns started, they harmonized beautifully — cowboy voices humble, raw, and earnest, filling the place like a warm wind rolling over prairie grass.

The pastor preached on humility.

"Pride bows for applause," he said. "But true humility bows for heaven."

Thomas whispered "Amen" so loud three pews jumped.

After service the bachelors hovered again, pretending to admire a fence post while eavesdropping. The Rangers ignored them, determined not to embarrass themselves, they mounted upon their horses. One boy tried to interrupt.

"So, uh, when's next trainin' sign-up—"

Boone froze him with a polite but suffering look. "Six months."

The boy whined, "But I wanna be refined too!"

Marshal clapped his shoulder. "Patience. Discipline. And biscuits."

The gatherers walked back to the boardinghouse — women leading with grace, men following at respectful pace on horseback, townsfolk whispering like bees in clover.

Hank whispered behind them, "I hope we get smaller portions this time."

Boone grabbed his elbow. "Do not say that where Maggie can hear. The Lord hears. But Maggie delivers."

They reached the house. The table gleamed. Biscuits rose. Tea steam curled. New lace napkins lay folded with heavenly promise.

Ellie turned, voice soft and sure. "Gentlemen, welcome to lesson two."

Their faces paled with reverence. And hunger. And terror.

Marshal whispered, "We shall endure."

Thomas whispered, "If we faint, bury us with dignity."

Boone groaned, "And with pie."

Naomi smiled graciously. "Let refinement begin."

And inside Providence, Missouri, heaven and humor met again, gently shaping hearts with scripture, flour, and patient purpose.

The storm had delivered them, but faith would do the building.

CHAPTER FIVE — GENTLE WORDS AND GENTLEMEN

Sunday sunshine lay soft as prayer across Providence, Missouri, shining through lace curtains in the Mercy Boardinghouse. Inside, the six women worked with quiet purpose, their movements steady and graceful, voices lowered to keep the peace of the Sabbath.

There had been laughter all week, yes, but now the mood was different—holy, expectant, like the hush right before a hymn begins. Lesson Two would require patience, and dignity, and prayer. Refinement was joy, yes, but it was also work.

Ellie tied her apron bow and smoothed it. "Ladies, we ask the Lord to steady us. These men are trying. They truly are."

Naomi nodded and folded her hands reverently. "Let us greet them with kindness. Gentle ways shape gentlemen."

Maggie wiped her hands on a cloth, flour dusting her fingers. "Amen. I'll be careful not to fuss over them if their collars go crooked."

Ruth Ann smiled faintly. "We will guide, not scold."

Lillian straightened a napkin at each place setting, her fingers lingering delicately. "And we will speak softly, as Scripture teaches."

Josie lit the last lamp, soft golden glow filling the room. "Let every word be seasoned with grace, that it may minister unto the hearers."

Colossians 4:6

"Amen," they murmured.

The table was set again with simple but beautiful dignity—china polished, linen smoothed, flowers from the yard arranged modestly in a jar. Bowls of biscuits sat waiting, steam curling like a gentle praise offering. Honey glistened in a small crystal dish. Sliced ham rested under a cloth. Butter sat molded neatly. There were greens, and stewed apples, and cornbread that smelled like memory and comfort.

Outside, slow hoof steps approached. Spurs chimed faintly. Men's voices murmured low.

Ellie looked at the others. "Steady hearts."

Maggie whispered, "Lord give them tongues ready for blessing and not stumbling."

A knock sounded. Ellie opened the door with calm grace.

The Rangers stood straight and solemn, hats in hand, their Sunday coats brushed and their expressions earnest. They looked like men arriving not to eat, but to learn how to be worthy.

Marshal inclined his head. "Good afternoon, ladies."

The women returned soft nods. Ellie stepped aside. "Please come in. Lessons begin with peace."

They entered, removing hats, smoothing jackets nervously. They sat when invited, posture stiff at first, then loosening a little as Naomi's gentle gaze reminded them no judgment lived here.

Ellie folded her hands on the table. "Today, we speak on how a gentleman greets a lady. When you approach, you do not demand attention. You do not startle. You announce your presence softly and offer respect."

She demonstrated a graceful nod.

Boone tried to mimic and nearly bowed too far before catching himself. He coughed once, recovering, while the women kept their faces charitable.

Marshal cleared his throat quietly. "Good afternoon, Miss Ellie. You look... blessed by the Lord this day."

Ellie inclined her head graciously. "Thank you kindly. That was thoughtful."

Hank swallowed. "Good evenin'—uh—good afternoon, Miss Naomi. Your dress... has got a gentle ribbon to it. I reckon it suits ya mighty well. Respectfully sayin'."

Naomi's smile was warm. "Thank you, Mr. Dawson. The Lord loves sweetness in speech."

Thomas breathed deeply, focusing as if reading scripture aloud. "Miss Lillian, may I say your manner today is peaceful as a Sabbath morning. And your hair is... arranged with honor."

Lillian's cheeks warmed delicately. "That is most gracious."

Carter turned toward Maggie, fingers gripping his hat brim tight. "Miss Maggie... your cookin' last week near brought me to tears of... holy appreciation. And you look very fine today... like a hymn baked fresh."

Maggie blinked, touched deeply. "Thank you kindly, sir."

Boone squared his shoulders, face red. "Miss Ruth Ann... I—uh—well—truth told, your way of speakin' is mighty even and calm. And there's somethin' real honorable in a woman who can keep a room steady."

Ruth Ann softened. "That is generous, Mr. Fletcher."

They finished rounds, the women praising each attempt, steadying awkward hands with gentle nods.

Ellie spoke quietly. "Now, we practice how a gentleman compliments without boasting nor flattery. Speak truth kindly, but do not invent beauty where you do not see it. God made every person with dignity, so speak to that dignity."

Marshal nodded slow. "Yes ma'am. I reckon truth wrapped polite is godly."

"Exactly," Ellie said. "Now, relax shoulders. Sit comfortably. A gentleman confident in his presence gives peace."

They attempted relaxation. Boone's chair creaked like it feared the responsibility. Carter inhaled deeply as though trying to breathe refinement. Hank exhaled shakily, then folded his hands like prayer anchored him in his seat.

Naomi set her voice calm as a hush before communion. "Let us pray grace."

Heads bowed.

Lord, bless this table, bless these hands, bless our learning and our listening. Shape us by Your peace. Give soft tongues and humble hearts. Let no pride live where You wish to dwell. And let our fellowship be pleasing in Your sight. Amen.

"Amen," they echoed softly.

Food was served. The women passed dishes with gentle grace. The men tried to maintain composure, but the first bite nearly undid them again. Warm biscuits melted like blessing. Ham salty and tender. Stewed apples sweet as Psalm-sung mercy.

Marshal whispered, voice reverent, "Lord forgive me… I forgot food had feelin's."

Boone exhaled slow and grateful. "I declare this is nourishment and comfort baptizin' my soul."

Thomas wiped his mouth gently. "This here is Proverbs woman cookin'."

Benn nodded solemn. "Above rubies."

The women served more, gentle smiles, refusing to tease or boast. Refinement had seriousness today. Responsibility. Godly hush.

Then, mid-meal, Marshal cleared his throat softly. "Ladies… if I may speak a query."

Ellie gestured for him to continue.

"How does a man… proper-like… get a say in matters? I mean, how does a man speak his thoughts around ladies without oversteppin', but not bein' silent neither?"

There was earnest confusion in his voice. His question carried the weight of future households, future shared decisions. It was honest. Noble. Vulnerable.

The women sat straighter.

Naomi spoke first, voice gentle as prayer. "A man's say is welcome when his spirit is humble. A woman does not fear a man's voice; she fears pride in it."

Thomas bowed his head. "That truth thunders quiet."

Ellie continued, "God made partnership. Men lead not with force, but with character. A man speaks after he listens. He guides without pushing. His strength makes space for a woman's wisdom."

Boone swallowed, thinking deeply. "So... you're sayin' a lady ain't meant to be hushed nor bossed, but respected. And she'll listen if the man got sense enough to speak kindly."

Ruth Ann nodded once. "Well said."

Marshal's gaze softened. "We aim to be men who guide without heavy hand."

"And we aim," Naomi replied, "to be women who honor good leadership."

Silence fell sweet as honey, not awkward but holy. Something in that moment settled, like seeds placed in good soil.

Ellie broke it gently. "Now continue your meal, gentlemen."

And the ladies served another round—big portions, warm plates refilled. The men did not refuse. They didn't know how to refuse. Pride had no space at this table; hunger and appreciation ruled instead.

Carter finally whispered, voice low and honest, "Miss Ellie, ma'am... if it ain't improper... may a man request to carry home somethin' left over, so he can think on the lesson with full stomach and a grateful heart?"

The women paused, then smiled, touched by his sincerity.

Maggie spoke softly. "Of course. We shall wrap something for each of you. Grace ought to go with you."

Hank nearly wept with relief. "Bless the Lord, oh my soul."

They continued eating, slower now, each bite thoughtful. Compliments came more naturally—gentle, sincere, reverent.

Boone murmured, "Miss Lillian, this bread... tastes like Sunday mornin' comfort."

She bowed her head modestly. "Thank you."

Thomas whispered, "Miss Josie, your table set like peace was laid out."

She smiled softly. "It is our joy to honor God with beauty."

Marshal paused with his fork mid-air. "Miss Ellie... every lesson you teach feels like buildin' more than manners. Feels like buildin' men."

Ellie's eyes warmed. "Good manners are simply goodness made visible."

Naomi added, "Scripture says, Be kindly affectioned one to another with brotherly love; in honor preferring one another."

Romans 12:10

"Amen," several voices whispered.

When plates were finally cleared and leftovers wrapped neatly in cloth bundles, Ellie stood. "We thank you for your effort today."

Marshal rose slowly, hand over heart. "We thank you for patience."

Carter bowed his head. "We shall carry these lessons with respect."

Boone clutched his biscuit parcel like treasure. "And we shall not waste one crumb."

Ruth Ann smiled gently. "May your week be fruitful."

The men put hats over their hearts, then turned to leave—walking slower, not from pain today, but from thoughtfulness. They mounted horses with decorum, each bundle tied carefully, as though it contained hope itself.

As they rode away, Naomi whispered, "See how the Lord molds?"

Ellie nodded. "Gentle pressure builds strong men."

And the women closed the door, not with triumph, but with humble peace. They had fed bodies, yes—but they had fed souls too.

Providence sunlight shone through the window, catching dust in holy dance.

Inside that old boardinghouse, laughter was quieter that day, replaced by reverence.

Where laughter plants friendship, stillness plants love.

And heaven, pleased, continued its quiet work.

The afternoon sun sat gentle on the dirt road as the Rangers stepped off the porch, their hats pressed to their chests in respectful farewell. Their boots struck the earth deliberate and steady. They mounted their horses with care, as though afraid a sudden move might shake loose the manners they had just been entrusted with.

Just as reins tightened and saddles creaked, a group of young town men ambled up, hats tipped low, curiosity thick as molasses in July.

"Howdy, fellas," one bachelor murmured, polite but nervous, like a man approaching a fence with a sleeping bull behind it. "We seen you comin' outta that boardin' house lookin' right proper. Wondered how them lessons goin'."

Marshal adjusted his hat brim, voice even. "They go decent. Women folks know refinement. We're learnin' steady."

A thin young clerk nodded too quickly. "Y'all... uh... eat good in there?"

Boone folded his arms across his chest, not unkind, but quiet as a tree that had seen many storms. "Good enough a man remembers it all week. That's all needs sayin'."

Another man swallowed hard. "So, uh... lessons worth it, you reckon?"

Carter kept his gaze easy. "Worth every word and every bite. No more talk on it."

And though no threat sat in their voices, the bachelors stepped back respectful, hats lowered further.

"Well," one said briskly, "we... hope we get our turn come winter."

Hank nodded once, gentle. "Refinement takes patience, friend. Your time'll come."

The group scattered then, whispers following on the dust, but soft and careful, for men who rode with old Texas steel in their bones commanded that sort of reverence without needing to raise tone nor fist.

The Rangers nudged horses forward, and hooves clopped slow down the road, each man sitting tall though the weight of biscuits and blessing pressed heavy in their middles once again.

Wind shifted through prairie grass as they reached open field. Boone loosened his collar. "Anybody else feel like they been filled from stomach to spirit both?"

Thomas released a weary groan. "I reckon I'm full clear to my eyelashes."

Hank held his parcel of leftovers tender as Sunday scripture. "I feel righteous... and plumb overfed."

Carter breathed deep. "But I ain't complainin'. A lesson that feeds both a man's mouth and his character is mercy from Heaven."

Benn nodded, slow and thoughtful. "Today weren't just food. It were direction. A man needs examples when tryin' to stand proper in his future home."

Marshal's voice softened like evening light. "Feels like the Lord fixin' to build somethin' in us. Somethin' worth comin' home to."

Back at the lodge, they dismounted with effort, groans escaping like prayers half-whispered.

Boone put a hand to his stomach. "If I die of good cookin' and gentle correction, bury me grateful."

Hank dragged a hand down his face. "Feels like sanctification sit heavy in my belly."

Carter untied his bundle, eyes shining. "And yet I ain't refusin' this supper. A man'd be a fool to turn down another taste of glory."

They laughed quietly, not wild like younger men, but steady and content, pain tucked beneath peace.

Thomas leaned against the porch beam. "Brothers... we needed this. Not just manners. Guidance. How to speak. How to honor. How to treat a home and a woman like somethin' the Lord Himself placed in our hands."

Marshal stared across pasture, voice low. "Next week we ask Reverend Thompson to come sit with us. Get a man's counsel alongside theirs. That way we shaped on both sides—Heaven through women's wisdom and Heaven through a shepherd's voice."

"Amen," Boone said.

"Amen," the others echoed.

They stepped inside, boots off, hats hung respectful, and sat heavy—worn not by hardship but by blessing too deep to rush through.

Outside the prairie stretched wide and golden, wind carrying faint scent of flour and hope from town.

Inside, six men rested in their chairs, sore in the belly, full in the soul, whispering tired prayers of gratitude before drifting into a peace that felt like new beginnings stitched by God's own hand.

CHAPTER SIX — WISDOM AT THE TABLE

Morning settled over Providence like a blessing poured slow from heaven's pitcher—calm, golden, and sure. The sun reached across the prairie, touching rooftops, horse barns, church steeple, and finally the hill where the Mercy Six boardinghouse stood watch over the little town like a patient guardian.

Inside the kitchen, gentle industry filled the air: the scrape of flour being sifted, the quiet clink of spoon against bowl, low hums of hymn tunes. The women moved peacefully, as though the Sabbath had never fully left the house.

Naomi murmured a short prayer as she stirred the grits. "Lord, give us a quiet spirit today. Teach us patience as we teach."

"Amen," Ellie whispered, arranging cups and saucers with reverence.

Lillian pressed fresh lavender sprigs on napkins, a soft, sacred touch.

Ruth Ann kneaded dough steady, firm, like shaping future homes.

Maggie basted ham slow, each brush stroke a hymn by itself. "Do y'all reckon the men practiced speakin' kind this week?"

Josie smiled as she poured coffee into the tall pot. "I believe they tried. A man don't endure pie-pain and etiquette elbow-aches unless he meant to grow."

Ellie folded her hands. "They asked for a reverend to attend. That shows humility."

Naomi nodded. "Humility is a garment God delights to see."

Ruth Ann dusted flour from her apron. "Pastor Thompson is comin' gentle. He said, 'I ain't there to judge nor correct—just to sit with my sons in the Lord and offer counsel if asked.'"

Josie sighed warm. "Bless him. A shepherd with a quiet staff."

Lillian placed a vase of prairie roses at center table. "Ladies, grace guides today. We calm the humor. We lift the reverence."

Maggie placed her wooden spoon down gently. "I'll try not to let my tongue run wild."

Ellie's lips curved. "A woman of Proverbs laughs, but she also discerns. Today we teach composure."

And just then—hoofbeats. Steady. Respectful. Not rushed, not boastful.

The men approached.

Marshal rode front, shoulders quiet, posture careful, eyes lowered like a man approaching church ground.

Behind him came Benn, Thomas, Carter, Boone, and Hank— shirts brushed, boots shined, hats clean, hair tamed best they knew how. They looked as if they had spent all week practicing not to tumble into foolishness.

Right beside them came the Reverend Ezra Thompson—old, silver-bearded, eyes like spring rain softening soil. He sat tall in the saddle but not proud. Age had bowed him in gentle ways, but his spirit remained upright as the oak trees lining Providence creek.

"Ladies," he greeted softly upon dismounting, removing his hat. "Peace of the Lord."

"And upon you, Reverend," Ellie replied with a grace that made the porch seem like a sanctuary.

The men stepped forward, hats in hand, boots quiet on the porch boards.

Boone cleared his throat softly. "Mornin', ladies."

Carter dipped his head. "We appreciate your time again."

Marshal spoke low and humble. "We ready to learn. And we brought Pastor Thompson to see us walk right."

The pastor chuckled low. "They asked me polite. I figured the Lord enjoys a good sight—men learnin' to be men in God's ways."

Naomi smiled. "You are welcome here, Reverend."

They entered, took seats at the table. The room felt like Sunday morning though service had already passed. Soft light glowed. Fresh bread blessed the air.

Ellie stood at the head. "Before we dine, we teach greeting."

She demonstrated again—chin slightly lowered, posture gentle, eyes warm, voice calm. "A gentleman greets a woman not as conquest nor obligation, but honor."

Marshal practiced. "Good afternoon, ma'am. You look peaceful today."

Ellie nodded. "Very well."

Boone tried next. "Good day, ladies. I pray y'all restin' well in the Lord."

Ruth Ann smiled. "Gracious tone, Boone. Slow, sincere."

Carter breathed steady. "Miss Maggie, thank you for openin' your home again. It feels right peaceful in here."

Maggie bowed her head faint, touched. "Thank you."

Hank whispered shy, "Miss Naomi, your presence looks restful today."

Naomi's heart warmed. "That is kind."

Thomas cleared his throat, wanting to honor. "Miss Lillian, your countenance shines calm. Scripture says a quiet spirit is of great worth before God."

Lillian's voice shook small and sweet. "Your words bless."

Benn nodded to Josie. "Ma'am, thank you for welcome. Table looks prepared with care."

Josie's eyes softened. "And we receive your gratitude."

Reverend Thompson watched, eyes shining proud. "Well done, boys. True courtesy begins in heart before mouth."

Ellie folded hands. "Now compliments."

They took turns again—soft, slow, steady—learning to see dignity where pride once blinded. Their phrases plain, their eyes earnest. Compliments not to flatter but to acknowledge godliness and effort.

The reverend nodded. "A house where peace dwells begins with how men speak."

Naomi recited softly, "A soft answer turneth away wrath." Proverbs 15:1

Boone whispered, "And a gentle word builds a strong woman."

Ruth Ann's breath caught—not romantic, but respectful. Growth is beautiful when seen.

Then Ellie gestured for plates. "Now relax shoulders. Gentle posture. Let your presence be comfort, not burden."

They exhaled in unison.

The pastor smiled. "Lord, look at these boys sittin' like saints in training."

Naomi bowed her head. "Grace before meal."

They prayed—not rushed, not dramatic—slow and humble:

Lord, form us into men and women who honor You first. Give soft tongues, patient hearts, and hands ready to build peace. Teach us how to tend homes, guard unity, and serve with quiet wisdom. Thank You for food and fellowship. Amen.

"Amen," breathed all.

And the meal began.

Not fast. Not foolish. Slow bites, soft conversation, reverent chewing. Ham tender, grits creamy, cornbread warm, collards seasoned just right, honey shining gold in lamplight.

Marshal closed his eyes a moment. "Miss Maggie... your hands bless the land."

Maggie blushed. "Glory goes to God."

Carter tasted apples and sighed. "Sweet as mercy."

Boone whispered over biscuits, "These here are humble enough a man remembers his place."

Reverend Thompson chuckled. "Food that makes a man grateful is holy."

Ellie guided, "Speak gently among yourselves. Share thoughts on household honor."

Marshal cleared his throat. "A man ought speak peace into his home. Not domination, not silence—peace."

Benn nodded. "A woman's spirit ought feel safe around her husband."

Thomas clasped hands. "And a man listens before speakin'. Scripture says be slow to speak and slow to anger."

Carter added, "And he prays before correctin' anything."

Boone chewed thoughtful. "And he don't bark commands like cattle orders."

Lillian whispered to the reverend, "They are learning."

He smiled kindly. "Men raised rough sometimes bloom softest under patience."

Naomi poured tea. "And may we, as women, build homes where men feel welcome to lead in humility. Partnership is not competition."

Maggie tapped her spoon slow. "We want homes where the Word lives louder than pride."

Josie nodded. "Where calmness, not noise, guides decisions."

Ruth Ann smoothed napkin edge. "Where no one wins arguments—only understanding wins."

Ellie finished gently. "Where strength protects peace, not destroys it."

For a moment, silence wrapped the table—a sacred hush.

The reverend wiped one eye. "Lord have mercy, I ain't never witnessed a classroom like this. Y'all teach Scripture without ever openin' a verse most times."

Naomi smiled. "We live the verse first."

Then came the moment the men had rehearsed with their horses as witnesses.

Marshal straightened softly. "Miss Ellie... I'd like to ask polite. Would it be acceptable for us to take some leftovers home? Not out of gluttony, but so we remember the lesson... and not go starvin' waitin' till next Sunday."

Lillian pressed hand to lips to hide warmth. Maggie nearly cried.

Ellie nodded soft. "Of course. There is blessing in what remains. We are glad to share."

Boone exhaled in relief so deep it was half prayer, half gratitude. "Thank the Lord. My insides ain't sure what to do with bein' full and humble at the same time."

The reverend laughed quiet. "Son, humility sits heavy sometimes. That's how you know it's real."

They finished the meal. Leftovers wrapped neatly in cloth, tied with twine, each parcel an act of care not charity.

When the men rose, hats in hand, Reverend Thompson wiped his beard and spoke soft as spring rain.

"My daughters in Christ, y'all are doin' a great holy work here. And you boys—give yourselves to this. A godly man ain't loud nor pushin'. He steady, he prayerful, he respectful. And when home comes, he guards it like a shepherd, not a sheriff."

Boone nodded. "Yes sir."

Carter whispered, "We takin' this serious."

Thomas added, "Feels like the Lord Himself teachin' through y'all."

Marshal looked Ellie in the eyes—not bold, not claimin', just grateful. "Thank you. For your patience and your trust."

Ellie bowed her head. "We are all learnin' under grace."

They stepped outside, still quiet, still full—of food, yes, but also purpose.

Young bachelors again lingered near street corner but said nothing this time; respect had grown roots.

The Rangers mounted. Saddles creaked softly. Sun dipped low like a benediction.

Hank whispered to Carter, "I feel different."

Carter nodded. "Better different."

Boone held his tin-wrapped bundle close. "Home's gotta be worth protectin' like this when God gives it."

Marshal looked back once, not to linger, but to honor. "Next week, we come ready heart and ready stomach, not boastin' nor slack."

The reverend chuckled. "And maybe smaller plates."

Thomas groaned. "Lord willing."

They rode slow toward their lodge, quiet men in thinking saddles.

Behind them the women watched a moment from the porch— soft smiles, warm eyes, no pride, only gratitude.

Maggie whispered, "Lord, they're growin'."

Naomi answered, "And so are we."

Ellie lifted her chin. "He buildeth the house."

And inside that little boardinghouse kitchen, the Spirit rested gentle as sleep on a newborn—unhurried, holy, and sure.

Refinement had become worship.

And Providence, Missouri, breathed peace.

CHAPTER SEVEN — A SEASON OF PAUSING

Five months had passed like soft wind over wheat — each week marked by quiet discipline, gentle correction, shared scripture, and a table where dignity fed discipline and biscuits fed courage. The boardinghouse, once worn and lonely, now lived. Curtains hung straight, floors shined, flowers sat in jars each morning like little prayers set in water. And though the Rangers had not laid a single board by their own hand, their ranch men had. Strong, respectful ranch hands, showing up steady every week with tools and quiet obedience, saying nothing of the masters who sent them, but always offering, always working.

The Mercy Six saw the truth: those men had chosen humility the only way they knew — by sending help in their stead while they learned how to be worthy enough to show up themselves someday.

The ranch hands had replaced planks, strengthened beams, mended rails, cleared brush, painted walls. They had left quietly before evening fell, tipping hats with shy thanks for cold lemonade and polite words, their eyes always carrying the message the Rangers could not speak: *We honor you. We are tryin', even if our pride keeps us back for now.*

And the women, wise enough to see it, never boasted. They prayed instead. Pride breaks slow, and they knew it.

But now word had come — not from riders' boots on the porch, not from Rangers clearing their throats at the door, hats between fingers, trying to gather courage. No. The men did not come.

Instead, the mayor and sheriff walked up the hill under clear sky, their steps respectful, their hats low, their shoulders bearing a message too heavy for pride to carry and too tender for mockery.

Ellie saw them through the lace curtain and felt her heart move holy and still.

Naomi whispered, "This is a season shifting."

Ruth Ann rested her hands on the parlor chair back. "We meet truth standing."

Maggie inhaled slowly. "The Lord prepares hearts."

Josie quieted her breathing. "We won't crumble. We pray."

Lillian smoothed her dress, chin lifting delicate. "We welcome truth gentle."

When the mayor knocked, Ellie opened the door calm, composed, eyes soft like Sunday morning after rain.

"Good afternoon," she greeted.

The sheriff removed his hat. "Ladies… we come with word from the Rangers."

Silence settled behind the women like a row of hymnbooks along a pew.

"They won't be makin' lessons for a while," the sheriff began, voice weighted, "and they asked us deliver the message on account that speakin' it to y'all direct felt too raw for them."

Maggie's hands twisted in her apron, but she kept her tone steady. "We hear you."

The mayor cleared his throat. "Roundup's comin'. Big one. Back acres flooded last year. Cattle scattered far. It's three months' work, maybe four. Hard work. Men don't get home often, and when they do, it's to fall asleep in their boots."

Lillian blinked slow. "We understand duty."

"They also say—" the sheriff paused, searching the room as though looking for the safest place to lay fragile truth, "—that preparin' weekly, dressin' proper weekly, carryin' themselves gentle weekly, it been... wearin' heavy on ranch time. They didn't complain. But they feel the strain."

Ellie's face softened. Not wounded — understanding. "They are torn between callings."

The mayor nodded. "They spoke grateful. Real grateful. Said y'all shaped 'em. Said lessons sat deep."

Josie's voice whispered like lace turning in wind. "But they go."

"They go," the sheriff affirmed.

A quiet fell so deep even the stove seemed to hush its warmth.

"They wanted y'all know they ain't quittin' in anger nor mockery," the mayor added. "They just... ain't ready to stand as men in front of you and say they need space."

Ruth Ann nodded once, firm but hurting. "Pride is a slow teacher."

"They'll ride day and night," the sheriff murmured. "The kind of tired that pulls sleep right down into the bones."

Naomi's voice came gentle. "We honor labor."

The mayor then spoke soft, almost reluctant. "They said... if someday y'all would be willin'... maybe you'd write again and help them find wives. Docile ones. Gentle ones. No questioning nor big plans nor schoolhouses nor business minds. Simple girls. Quiet girls who don't push nor pull."

The women did not gasp nor stiffen nor show pain with loudness. They received truth like noble women do — standing upright, hearts bowed but not broken.

Lillian spoke first, voice small but sure. "They still desire women untroubled by ambition."

"Yes ma'am," the sheriff whispered. "That's what they think they want."

Maggie's throat moved but she said nothing harsh. "Comfort ain't always covenant."

Naomi placed a hand over her chest. "They want ease, not

partnership yet. It is not sin. It is simply immaturity."

Ellie breathed slow, one steady breath. "When the Lord calls, we write. But we shall not send lambs into houses that desire silence more than strength."

The mayor swallowed hard. "They ain't seein' clear yet. But I believe they will. Time does God's work."

Ruth Ann nodded gently. "And we do not chase what God pauses."

"They are not free from affection," the sheriff added softly. "Don't think they ride off glad. They hurt too."

Naomi whispered, "Then may God comfort both sides."

The sheriff bowed his head. "You're good women. They know it."

"We are God's women," Ellie corrected kindly. "He knows it."

The men stepped back. "We'll leave you to prayer."

And they left, boots quiet, hats low, leaving silence like snowfall — soft, cold at first, then settling.

Inside, the Mercy Six stood still, dignified grief resting on them like a shawl worn at a funeral.

Maggie's voice trembled barely. "It aches."

Josie nodded, eyes wet. "I didn't expect it to ache, but it does."

Lillian whispered, "Is it foolish to feel attached when no promise was given?"

Naomi stepped close, touching her hand. "Attachment is not sin. Hope is not weakness."

Ruth Ann's voice held steady sorrow. "And disappointment is not failure."

Ellie lifted her chin. "We do not cling to men. We cling to purpose. God's hand did not stop movin'. Only human plans paused."

They moved into prayer circle without needing to speak the need.

Ellie began. "Lord, bless their labor."

Naomi added. "Guard their bodies and humble their fears."

Maggie whispered. "Turn pride like soil ready for seed."

Ruth Ann breathed. "Let time do what lessons begun."

Josie said softly. "And hold their hearts as You hold ours."

Lillian closed. "Teach us patience without bitterness."

Silence covered prayer like a quilt.

Then they opened their eyes — not with despair, but resolved sorrow.

"Back to work," Ellie said softly.

And they went — to knead bread slow, sew straighter seams than yesterday, sweep floors until boards shone again, and water flowers by the porch where hope waited patiently in clay soil.

Far across the prairie, dust rose as six silhouettes rode long trail lines. They did not hoot nor holler. No songs today. Only quiet, like men carrying both duty and ache in saddlebags.

Boone murmured, "Feels wrong ridin' away without a word."

Carter swallowed. "Couldn't form the words if we tried."

Marshal kept his eyes forward. "We plan on comin' back better. God ain't finished."

Thomas wiped his cheek quick, pretending dust. "Pride's a stubborn mule. But so's love, when it's God-led."

Hank clutched his food parcel like comfort scripture. "They deserve men who ain't afraid of strong women."

Benn exhaled long. "Lord, don't let us waste what they poured."

They rode farther, sun gold around them, cattle lowing in distance, ranch calling like a duty that does not check emotion first.

The Mercy House behind remained still and shining, windows bright though hearts inside felt tender bruising.

God was not breaking anything.

He was **stretching**.

And Heaven whispered over fields and hills and saddles and

flour-dusted aprons:

Not goodbye.
Just not yet.

CHAPTER EIGHT — CALLED FORWARD

The days that followed felt long and low, like walking through tall grass after the rain—beauty there, yes, but heaviness brushing every step. Morning light still came through the boardinghouse windows gentle and gold, but the laughter that once filled the kitchen now lay quiet as folded linens on Sunday afternoon.

The Mercy Six worked. They baked. They stitched. They polished floors. They sold biscuits, bread, pies, and small sewn linens to townsfolk who came with soft voices and sympathetic glances. But each smile felt stretched, each greeting spoke through a veil of ache. Business went on, as life does, but hearts moved slower than hands.

In the first week after the men rode out, Naomi would pause over her kneading bowl, breath catching mid-prayer. Ruth Ann found herself wiping the same shelf twice though it was already clean. Lillian lingered by the window longer than needed as though expecting dust clouds or silhouettes. Maggie stirred batter slower than her usual lively rhythm, as if stirring memory too. Josie smoothed tablecloth edges like smoothing grief that refused to lay flat. Ellie kept her posture straight, her voice steady, but even steel can ache beneath polish.

They had not meant to fall in love. They had meant only to teach. To labor for the Lord. To guide young men toward gentleness and dignity. To offer refinement in obedience. Yet love sometimes blooms in service, quietly and without permission, like wild roses along fences where no gardener planned for beauty.

They had felt something growing, not childish nor trivial. Not only admiration for strong shoulders bowed in prayer or rough hands holding teacups carefully. Not only softness stirred when a man bowed awkwardly but sincerely, or when his voice trembled trying to compliment modestly. It had been the tenderness of watching men try. The ache of seeing pride bend. The wonder of witnessing hearts reach toward virtue. That had been the falling.

And now the absence of that trying felt like standing at a quiet grave—not of death, but of possibility buried before bloom.

They did not speak of love directly. But grief showed itself in small ways. Maggie's laughter, once bright as butter in sunlight, now came quieter, slower, as though rising through thick sorrow first. Naomi lingered longer on prayer each dawn, fingers tight around her Bible edge, whispering as though asking God to hold what she couldn't name. Ellie walked the house as though inspecting strength, yet her breaths sometimes hitched in hallways where memory hung like lace.

They served. They smiled politely. They worked. They prayed.

Yet in kitchen corners and attic rooms, tears stitched silent lines into fabric and flour. Not dramatic sobs—no, these were grown women, emotionally anchored by God, not swayed by mere longing. But hearts do not cease feeling simply because they know holiness. Tears came quiet, private, like a confession only the Lord needed to hear.

Two weeks passed.

Then, one still morning while dawn hatched pink across sky, a rider brought a letter, sealed in blue wax, bearing the Mercy College crest. Naomi opened the door with flour still on her hands, hair pinned back neat but tired, and the envelope trembled lightly as it was pressed into her palm.

She called softly, "Ladies... there is post from Pennsylvania."

Every woman paused mid-chore. Maggie set down her spoon. Ruth Ann stilled her broom. Josie stopped lacing her apron. Lillian turned from arranging flowers. Ellie lifted her head from the ledger book where figures waited to be reconciled.

Naomi brought the letter to the kitchen table. They gathered around it like around a prayer request or a sacred invitation. Ellie broke the seal with steady hands though her heart thumped like running feet.

She read slowly, her voice gaining strength with each sentence:

To our honored Mercy graduates,
Heroes of your calling and daughters of our faith,

It is with joy and urgency that we write. Mercy College has been granted funds to expand our ladies' instruction wing. We are beginning construction of a new Hall of Domestic Arts and Refined Trades. We request your return to lead curriculum design and instruction.

We need you.

Come home to build the future.

Your salaries shall commence immediately, and lodging prepared. We await your affirmative answer with gladness and prayer.

Signed,
Dean Whitaker
Mercy College for Ladies
Pennsylvania

Ellie finished. Silence fell, but this silence was not like the one left by departing men. This silence pulsed. It breathed. It glimmered like morning dew catching sunlight.

Then Maggie gasped. Not sorrow—astonishment. The first spark in her eyes since the men rode out. "They need us."

Lillian covered her mouth, tears rising but these were bright, not salt-heavy. "The Lord did not forget."

Ruth Ann exhaled, strength filling her posture. "We are wanted for what we studied. For what God planted."

Naomi clasped her hands under her chin. "He never leaves His daughters without purpose."

Josie let out a soft, stunned laugh. "Oh, bless His holy name."

Ellie closed her eyes, tears welling but unshed—steady tears, grateful ones. "We are called forward."

In one moment, heaviness lifted. Like fog burned off by sudden sunrise. Grief loosened its grip. Hearts that had been curled inward unfurled again like petals touching warmth.

Ellie spoke first with calm resolution. "We go."

Maggie nodded, breath lifting. "We go."

Naomi's eyes shined like morning prayer answered. "We go."

Josie pressed a hand to her chest. "This is Providence."

Ruth Ann tightened her jaw, determined strength back in her spine. "This was always part of the story."

Lillian whispered, voice trembling with peace. "He did not let us be discarded. He hid us for a moment, preparing to lift us."

They moved with purpose now—light packing, quiet folding, respectful leaving. No dramatic goodbyes. No carriage parade. They did not seek town eyes nor sympathy.

They left a note pinned gently on the boardinghouse door:
Closed. Mercy College has called. We follow the Lord's next work.

They left another at the lawyer's door:
Please sell the boardinghouse on our behalf. We shall contact you in due time.

And that was all. No need to explain. No need to defend hearts. The men had chosen silence for their season, so the women chose silence for theirs. Not in bitterness—but in dignity.

They prepared departure in three days. The town noticed only the last morning when trunks appeared outside, modest and neatly tied. Mrs. Brewer from the general store wiped her eyes discreetly when she saw them. The pastor's wife pressed Bibles into their hands as blessings. A few brothers from church helped lift trunks without asking where or why—they knew calling when they saw it.

And as the stagecoach rattled up that last hill, horses snorting gentle steam into morning chill, the Mercy Six lifted their skirts, boarded one by one, and settled inside as though stepping not away from loss, but into destiny.

Josie leaned toward the window, voice soft. "Do you reckon they'll hear we're gone?"

Ruth Ann answered quietly, "When God wishes."

Maggie looked down at her hands. "Do you think they cared?"

Ellie touched her arm—gentle, firm. "We loved. They were not ready. God does not waste love; He stores it for seasons yet to bloom."

Naomi added, "And there is no shame in loving. Only in forsaking your calling for it."

Lillian whispered, "We did not lose. We were redirected."

The coach jerked forward. Wheels rolled. Providence shrank behind them. But hope stretched ahead wider than prairie sky.

No mournful weeping. No slammed hearts. Just quiet ache turning to quiet faith. And as fields gave way to horizon, the Spirit whispered in six hearts at once:

Daughters, you obeyed. Now go build nations.

And like seed carried on wind, they left—heads high, hearts healing, stepping into the future Mercy had always meant.

CHAPTER NINE — THE YEAR OF WAITING AND WORKING

The stagecoach rattled down the hill away from Providence, wheels cutting through morning frost. Inside it, six women sat straight-backed, hands folded atop skirts, expressions calm though hearts beat uneven rhythms. Dust rose behind them like memory trying to follow.

At the foot of the hill waited the train station—the same iron road that had once carried them westward dreaming of farmland, school rooms, bakeries, and homes built with laughter and work and love born by God's hand. Now it would carry them east—toward the life they had prepared for before love had brushed their hearts quiet and unexpected.

"Funny," Maggie murmured softly, not with humor but with wonder. "We came chasin' purpose and found it here, then found it again leavin'."

Naomi touched her hand. "Purpose travels. It does not stay still."

Ellie looked out the coach window, jaw set in resolve. "And calling does not ask permission from feelings."

Ruth Ann folded her gloves neat. "Hearts heal faster when hands stay busy."

Josie exhaled. "Mine ain't healed yet."

"Nor mine," Lillian whispered.

Ellie rested her palm over both of theirs. "We follow God, not grief."

The stage stopped. The train hissed steam. They stepped down one by one—modest trunks, lace gloves, quiet dignity. They did not rush. They did not tremble. They moved like women stepping into destiny again.

As the whistle blew, Naomi whispered a scripture, voice low:

"The Lord shall perfect that which concerneth me."
Psalm 138:8

They boarded. Windows framed their silhouettes—six women sitting upright with sorrow behind them and God ahead. As the train groaned forward, Providence shrank to a memory painted in soft colors. They did not wave back. No one stood there to see them off.

The whistle cried long across plains. So did six hearts, silently.

The train rolled.

And life turned another page.

Back in Providence — Two weeks later

Dust swirled in the ranch yard. Noon sun beat warm. The Rangers rode in from far back pasture—calloused hands, tired eyes, horses lathered from hours of cattle driving.

Marshal lifted his head. "Feels like a quiet day in town."

Boone wiped sweat off his brow. "Might ride in tomorrow. Say a proper hello."

Hank smiled faintly. "Be good to sit proper again. Eat proper— maybe hear Miss Maggie pray over biscuits."

Thomas grinned, hopeful but cautious. "We walk in clean, mind our manners, bow right. Show 'em we ain't the same fools."

Benn nodded slow. "And maybe... maybe we ask if they still teach on patience."

Carter smiled like it hurt. "And if they still—"

Hoofbeats interrupted. Sheriff Porter rode in, hat low, face solemn.

All men straightened, hearts already tightening.

He dismounted slow. Looked at them. Cleared his throat. Removed hat. Voice low as dirt prayer.

"They're gone."

Marshal's breath caught sharp. "Gone?"

"Left two weeks ago. Took the stage. Caught the eastbound train. Boardinghouse shuttered. Note says Mercy College called them back."

Silence slapped hard.

Boone stared like someone cut rope beneath him. "They left?"

Sheriff nodded. "Quiet. Dignified. Didn't tell a soul. Left a note with the lawyer to sell the house."

Hank blinked, stunned. "Why so sudden?"

"They felt... released," the sheriff answered. "Their calling opened. School wants 'em. Needs 'em."

Carter's jaw clenched. "So that's it?"

Thomas whispered, voice shaking, "We rode out thinkin' they'd wait."

Naomi's earlier words returned unbidden: *We shall not send lambs into houses that desire silence more than strength.*

Marshal shook his head slow. "We left. We chose work. They chose callin'. Ain't nobody wrong. Ain't nobody right. Just time."

Boone turned away, boots heavy in dust. "We wanted life easy. And they ain't easy."

Sheriff spoke gentle. "They are righteous women. God led 'em. That's all."

Hank whispered, "We should've told 'em thank you in person."

Thomas wiped his face. "We should've told 'em more'n that."

Marshal finally found breath, though it broke inside him. "We ain't ready. They saw it. We saw it. Lord ain't cruel. He just ain't careless."

Silence again.

They stood as men do when heartbreak visits—quiet, stunned, still trying to be strong in front of one another.

Then the sheriff rode away.

And six men stood in ranch dust like statues carved from regret and awakening.

Boone said first, voice raw. "I didn't know missin' someone could feel like bein' kicked in the ribs slow."

Carter swallowed. "Do we ride after 'em?"

Marshal shook his head. "Not now. Men don't chase what God ain't released 'em to hold. We work. We grow. We pray. We wait God's say-so."

Thomas murmured, "A wife ain't somethin' you go chasin' when you still halfway boy."

Benn exhaled heavy. "Pride cost us this season."

Hank closed eyes. "Lord, grow us up."

They turned back toward cattle fields—not with swagger, but with holy sorrow.

Seasons end. Seasons return.

They would not forget.

Six Months Later — Mercy College, Pennsylvania

Snow fell like lace from heaven over Mercy College's new wing under construction. The halls buzzed with learning again—girls with books and hope, sewing needles clicking, bread rising in ovens, laughter young and bright, future stirring everywhere.

The Mercy Six walked the polished corridors with dignity. Their voices carried wisdom now, not simply instruction. They taught budgets and bread, dignity and domesticity, literature and living by faith.

They were not just teachers. They were builders.

Every evening, they gathered in their shared parlor—sewing,

sipping tea, writing lessons. Their grief did not vanish; it softened. It turned into memory shaped like prayer.

Ellie drafted curriculum on leadership for women.
Naomi wrote devotionals for students.
Maggie tested recipes for school kitchens.
Ruth Ann organized ledgers with strict excellence.
Josie taught hospitality and speech.
Lillian led etiquette circles that reminded her of six humble cowboys trying to sit proper at lace-covered tables.

Sometimes she'd pause, needle in hand, breath held like glass.

And Maggie would whisper, "Still miss 'em?"

Lillian would nod, eyes warm with both ache and peace. "Miss what they were tryin' to be more than what they were."

Ellie always closed such moments with Scripture:

"They that wait upon the Lord shall renew their strength."
Isaiah 40:31

And they did.

Meanwhile — Providence, Missouri

Winter dusted the ranch. The men worked harder than ever —branded cattle in snow, prayed by firelight, read etiquette notes by lamplight like scripture, spoke softer to ranch hands, practiced patience with ornery calves and ornery tempers. They sat straighter. They ate slower. Some nights, Boone read Proverbs aloud over his stew.

Marshal carved wood quietly by the fire—little roses into fence rails, not knowing why.

Thomas preached to the men sometimes—gentle sermons about humility and being worthy of blessing.

Carter wrote letters he never mailed.
Hank prayed under the stars.
Benn set aside money each month— "for a future home worth her."

And every Sunday they sat in the front pew, not to be seen, but because they needed God now like never before.

Pastor preached one morning, voice calm:

"Sometimes God don't say no. He say not yet."

The men closed eyes.

They understood seasons now.

One Year Later Since the Women Left

It was spring again in Missouri. Prairie grass came green, newborn calves bawled, sun warmed the lodge porch. The men stood outside, hats off, shirts clean, posture straight not from etiquette but from manhood ripening under God.

Marshal looked toward the empty hill far beyond. "Year gone."

Boone nodded. "Feels longer."

Carter said, almost to himself, "Wonder if they forgot us."

Thomas shook his head. "Good women don't forget seeds planted."

Benn exhaled. "World don't feel full without them."

Hank whispered, "Lord, if You ever let us cross paths again, let it be as men who don't ask women to shrink to fit our fear."

And heaven listened.

Across states and miles and seasons, at Mercy College, Naomi paused in her office. She closed her Bible gently and whispered:

"Lord, if they grow into men worthy of covenant, lead them back. But if not, lead us forward still."

And heaven listened.

A year had passed. Hearts still stitched to purpose. Pain softened into prayer. Pride turned into quiet soil waiting for God to plant what He chose.

They did not chase.
They did not forget.
They trusted holy timing.

Sometimes love grows loud.
Sometimes it grows waiting.

God was not done.

He was preparing.

CHAPTER TEN — THE LORD SENDS US BACK

A year had rolled like wheat bowing under seasons. The Mercy Six had grown into pillars at Mercy College, respected by faculty and beloved by students. The new Domestic Arts Wing, once only drawings and dreams, now stood grand—brick shining, windows tall, voices of young women inside like hymns of future promise.

Day after day, the Mercy Six walked these halls with poise God Himself stitched into them. They taught more than domestic arts—they taught dignity, courage, prayer, and purpose.

It was early spring when a carriage finer than any they had seen pulled up to Mercy College. Two black horses, polished harnesses, gold-trimmed doors. The steward stepped down and said:

The Honorable Mr. Alderton requests audience with the Mercy graduates.

Alderton was whispered about: a shipping magnate, philanthropist, friend to congressmen, a man who believed women's education strengthened families and nations. His arrival felt like a chapter turning.

In the dean's sitting room, with tea steaming and sunlight warming lace curtains, Mr. Alderton rose when the Mercy Six entered. He bowed slightly—not theatrical, but respectful.

Ladies, he said with deep sincerity, I have followed your work. You built this wing not only with knowledge, but with spirit. You are what education ought to be. And our nation needs more of you.

Ellie inclined her head. Sir, we only did what we were called to do.

He smiled. Some callings echo far. It is time yours reached beyond Pennsylvania.

He laid a map across the table. The women leaned closer. Their hearts stilled as his finger tapped a spot on the paper.

Missouri.

Ellie's breath paused.

Near Providence, Mr. Alderton continued, unaware of the tension he stirred. Five miles east. Land donated by a benefactor who desires to cultivate Christian women of intelligence, dignity, and purpose.

The room held its breath.

Ruth Ann felt blood rush to her ears. Josie's fingers gripped her skirt. Maggie swallowed, throat suddenly dry. Naomi pressed one palm against her Bible. Lillian steadied herself by gripping the chair back lightly.

We would like you six to establish and lead this school, he said with pride. You will have full authority, generous salary, housing, and staff. If you accept, you must depart within three months. Construction begins immediately.

They stared at him—women who had learned obedience costs breath sometimes.

He smiled, assuming shock but not knowing its depth. Pray on it, he said kindly. I shall expect your answer soon.

He bowed again, left his card, and departed in carriage splendor.

The door shut.

Silence did not fall. It descended.

Naomi whispered first. Providence.

Ruth Ann shook her head slowly. Five miles. Only five.

Josie's hands trembled. Lord, strengthen us.

Maggie pressed fingers to her lips. After all this time.

Lillian slowly sank into a chair. Too close.

Ellie stood very still, eyes lowered, then lifted slowly toward heaven. God, what are You doing with us?

For hours they sat. Not speaking much. Their breaths held grief and astonishment both.

Finally Ellie said, We must pray.

And they knelt—not on polished church kneelers, but on the college's wooden floor, skirts brushing dust motes that danced in sunbeams.

Naomi prayed first. Lord, we serve You. Only You. We return nowhere for flesh's sake. We follow calling, not memory.

Maggie cried softly. Father, I do not know if my heart can bear it.

Josie whispered, I fear seeing them and not being seen.

Ruth Ann breathed, And I fear seeing them changed and being seen too much.

Lillian murmured, I fear returning to hope.

Ellie closed her eyes. Lord, we left because You called. Shall we return because You call again?

Silence.

Then a scripture rose in Ellie's spirit like breath after drowning.

Return to the land, for there I will deal kindly with you.
Genesis 32:9

She did not speak it aloud yet. She held it like a seed.

When they rose, their skirts rustled like leaves in wind. Their faces glowed not with certainty but with surrender.

We have time, Ellie said softly. We do not rush what God has not rushed.

Three days later, letters came from Providence. The mayor's handwriting.

Ellie read aloud by lamplight.

Dear ladies,

Word reached us you are thriving. Providence remembers you kindly.

The Rangers continue well. Working, attending church, conducting themselves upright.

They have sought assistance in procuring mail-order wives. They request women stout in form, gentle in nature, quiet in spirit, not questioning nor ambitious.

Thus far, no one has succeeded in writing such description.

Maggie's chest hurt as if someone pressed a fist there.

The letter continued:

Some say they are particular to the point of stubbornness. Others say hurt has stiffened them. The town believes they never recovered fully from your sudden departure. They think themselves betrayed. They guard their hearts.

Ellie paused. Her hand shook once. Then she read:

Yet they are regarded as good men. Tired men. Proud men trying to grow. They speak not of love now. Only duty. The pastor says the Lord will soften what sorrow has hardened.

Ruth Ann closed her eyes. Lord, help them.

They listened to the end:

If ever you return, Providence will welcome you. The hills remember your footsteps.

The room went still again.

Josie whispered, We broke something when we left.

Naomi shook her head softly. No. We obeyed God. Their breaking came from pride, not abandonment.

But the ache was real. They felt it like a bruise that never fully faded.

Weeks passed. They taught. They prayed. They packed slowly, then unpacked, then packed again—hearts unsettled like travelers standing in two worlds.

One evening in late summer, Naomi rose in prayer circle with trembling voice.

I dreamed we returned. The men did not run to us nor turn away. They stood and watched us like men waiting on God not on longing. They looked older. Sober. They had learned patience.

Maggie's eyes filled. Did they... look happy?

Naomi hesitated. They looked ready.

Ruth Ann whispered, Ready for God or ready for us?

Naomi answered, I could not tell. Or perhaps the Lord meant both.

Silence. Deep. Holy.

Ellie finally spoke: We must not fear God's assignments because they brush old wounds. We go where He sends, not where comfort lies.

Josie breathed, but what if obedience hurts again?

Then Ellie quoted softly:

They that sow in tears shall reap in joy.
Psalm 126:5

Maggie closed her Bible gently. We go then?

Lillian whispered, if we must stand near love again and not touch it, will our hearts survive?

Ruth Ann answered firm, If God sends us, He sustains us.

Naomi nodded. To refuse His call is to refuse His comfort also.

Ellie stood tall, eyes steady with obedience. We will say yes.

They did not shout. They did not weep loud. They simply exhaled—like letting go of self-one last time.

At year's close, they wrote:

To the Honorable Mr. Alderton,
We accept.
In Christ's service,
The Mercy Ladies

Packing began again—not rushed, not fearful, but reverent. They folded gowns and lesson plans. They gathered cooking tools and embroidery frames. They prayed over every trunk and tied each ribbon with purpose.

Maggie paused once, pressing a shawl to her chest.

Naomi asked, Sad?

Maggie smiled thin but real. Sad and hopeful often walk hand in hand.

Naomi nodded. Yes. Like faith and waiting.

Ellie looked toward the horizon through the dormitory window. Providence waited. The ranch waited. Whether hearts there softened or hardened further was God's business.

Ours is obedience, she whispered.

And so they prepared to go back—not for men, not for romance, but for God's will, whether blessing or testing waited beyond those hills.

Love had not vanished. But calling came first.

And courage rose again because obedience demanded it.

CHAPTER ELEVEN — THE SETTLERS WHO CAME QUIET

Autumn drifted gentle across Missouri, painting hills copper and gold. Providence town breathed its usual rhythm, slow but steady—church bells on Sundays, wagons creaking past with flour sacks, children running down dusty lanes with straw-doll braids bouncing. Life did not pause simply because hearts once had broken and were learning slow to heal.

Beyond town, beyond the ridge where wind whispered secrets only God heard, six ranch homes stood untouched, their owners riding long fields each day, working cattle, praying in quiet, and strengthening souls for whatever season Heaven had next.

And then—before the Mercy Ladies returned, before the Lord's plan showed its next turn—something unexpected stirred on the horizon.

One crisp morning, dust rose far off—steady, heavy, moving like a low cloud crawling across earth. Children in town shaded their eyes. Storekeepers paused sweeping stoops. Horses lifted heads.

It was a wagon caravan—dozens deep, canvas tops bowed, oxen slow and true, families walking beside wheels. Psalm-singing voices floated faint on breeze, steady and unbroken like a long prayer made of human footsteps.

Old Mr. Finch at the feed store leaned forward squinting. "Well I'll be. Looks like the Abraham folks."

Pastor's wife Mrs. Hale lowered her spectacles. "Who?"

"A settlin' sect," Mr. Finch murmured. "God-fearing types. Heard of 'em tin Kansas Territory. Quiet folk. Devoted. Don't allow foolishness nor idle tongues."

The wagons rolled closer, each marked with neat painted text:

House of Refuge and Promise Colony
Holiness unto the Lord

Women rode in quiet posture—hands clasped, bonnet ribbons tied firm, backs straight, heads bowed just enough not to challenge the horizon. They were strong of arm and broad of shoulder, built by labor not vanity, flesh soft with baking and kneading and carrying wood, not with idleness.

They were curvy—full-hipped, broad-bosomed, sturdy as kitchen tables, built to stand and work and endure. But their faces held no mischief, no sparkle of teasing spirit, no free laughter waiting to burst. They were serene, solemn, trained in gentle silence.

Their kin folk walked beside them with Bibles tucked close. Their fathers walked straight-backed with rifles over shoulders but eyes soft with reverence. Children hummed scriptural songs instead of play tunes. No ribbons fluttered. No skipping steps. Obedience marched with them like a standard.

By the time they reached the town square, the pastor had stepped out, Bible under his arm. The sheriff tipped his hat. Store windows filled with curious faces.

The lead wagon stopped. Out stepped Elder Abram Holt—tall, beard trimmed modest, coat plain but well-cared, eyes deep with conviction as a winter well.

"Peace to this place," he said warm but firm. "We come in the Lord's name. Seeking homestead land to settle and honor God by labor."

Pastor Hale nodded respectful. "Peace be multiplied unto you. Providence welcomes Christian souls."

The townsfolk gathered close, listening as Elder Holt explained: they came from a community westward, grown too crowded. They chose new soil, believing God wanted them to plant faith in fresh ground. Four homestead parcels had been secured through a land agent week earlier—fertile plains not far from a ranching block belonging to six respected cowboys known for hard work and honorable dealings.

The town shared glances. Everybody knew who those six were.

And so, arrived the new women—thirty daughters and relatives in all, ages sixteen to twenty-eight, raised in scripture, trained in obedience, taught homemaking like it was gospel—baking, sewing, child-tending, dairying, gardening, modest speech, submission as sacred duty.

They were everything those Rangers thought they wanted. Everything the Mercy Six were not.

At least… on the surface.

For obedience without joy makes a heart quiet as winter bark. Submission without spirit makes a voice soft as cloth. The Lord did not design womanhood small, but this colony believed stillness holier than song, and duty safer than laughter.

Pastor Hale offered lodging help. Town mothers brought quilts. But even hospitality could not soften the solemn order in which these women moved, heads bowed, skirts rustling like whispered scripture.

Whispers floated around storefronts that evening:

"They're mighty serious."

"Pious like angels."

"Not a giggle nor glimmer in one."

"They will make fine wives."

"Fine? Perhaps. But will they make a life?"

Elder Holt overheard none of it. He only spoke blessings, thanking townsfolk and requesting direction to the ranchlands.

Deputy Callum cleared his throat. "Those parcels sit right near the Franklin spread. You'll pass the lands of those six ex-Texas Rangers."

A hush. The settlers had heard of them already—stories came long before wagons rolled. Rumors of strong men, wealthy by ranching, god-fearing, tall, sturdy, quiet, leaders among cattle and land.

A few of the curvy disciplined daughters lifted their heads just a little—not enough to break modesty, but enough to show human curiosity not yet trained out.

Elder Holt clasped hands in prayer posture. "We seek godly neighbors. Men who honor duty. The Lord may bless our daughters with such."

Some town women shared glances. Somber wives for somber men? Would that bind joy or build home? Time alone would tell.

They moved on—settling at their parcels, laying tents, then setting axes to wood with sober diligence. They prayed before meals, after meals, before building, after building. They sang at night only hymns in minor key, no playful tunes.

And five miles away on six ranches, six men unsaddled after a long day, unaware new lives had just pitched canvas near their fences.

Unaware eyes would soon watch them from afar with hope, prayer, and trained submission.

Unaware God was weaving threads they did not expect.

For though these settlers brought virtue, they brought also shadows: belief that women should not speak unless spoken to. That a cheerful wife invited sin. That strength in a woman meant something dangerous rather than divine.

Providence braced. Heaven watched.

And in Pennsylvania, six women in a brick dormitory folded lesson plans for Christian young ladies, unaware strangers now stood wanting futures near their men.

The Mercy Ladies still prayed nightly for strength to return.

They did not know rivals had been planted first. They did not know God was testing alignments, showing the Rangers what they thought they wanted.

Those solemn daughters looked toward ranch hills with hope.

But the living God prepares hearts before He reunites stories.

As Elder Holt's people prayed over campfires, and the Mercy Six packed trunks far away, and the Rangers brushed down horses under orange sunset unaware—

Angels stood at corners of the map
holding breath
waiting to move pieces when the Father spoke one word:

Soon.

CHAPTER ELEVEN — THE SUBMIT & SERVE FELLOWSHIP

Autumn settled over Missouri like a shawl stitched in gold and rust. Providence moved in its slow rhythm—church bells, children playing, smoke drifting from chimneys, wagon wheels rattling over rutted roads. Nothing seemed restless. Nothing seemed urgent. Only the steady hum of life.

Then, one crisp morning, dust stirred far down the eastern trail —thick and rising, like a slow-coming storm. Farmers shaded their eyes. Mothers paused hanging wash. The pastor felt his heart pause in his chest, though he did not yet know why.

A caravan approached—wagons in solemn procession, oxen steady, banners painted with verses of submission and obedience. The words looked holy to uncareful eyes. But the wind, wise to spirits, seemed to sigh through them instead of carry them.

The first wagon bore its name bold across white canvas:

Submit & Serve Fellowship
Holiness. Modesty. Obedience.

Heads turned. Whispers fluttered like startled sparrows.

"They're devout folk," murmured Mrs. Kepper at the mercantile.

"Or they want us to think so," Mr. Finch muttered under his breath. His eyes narrowed. Age sometimes sees what youth misses.

The wagons stopped in the square. Men stepped down—stern faces, rigid postures, clothes plain but too uniform, too exact. Their Bibles tucked like weapons of power, not worship.

Their women stepped down next—husband's eyes watching every movement. They were strong, curvy women, sturdy from labor and farm living. Built like hearths—able to bear heat, work, and burden.

But there was like they were trained to have **no laughter** in them. No spark. No lifted joy.

Only practiced serenity, stillness drilled deep as a rule—not a virtue.

They were quiet, heads bowed, hands folded. Not humility—**compliance**.

Pastor Hale greeted the leader, Elder Marcus Bane. The man bowed with stiff politeness, his voice smooth as butter churned without sweetness.

"Peace of the Lord from the Submit & Serve Fellowship."

The pastor offered a gentle welcome, but unease flickered in his eyes.

"And what brings you here, Elder Bane?"

"Opportunity and obedience," Bane replied. "We seek a place to spread holy living. A land to raise God-fearing children. To plant righteousness."

He spoke like scripture—yet it felt like stone.

Behind him, young women stood still as fence posts, eyes lowered. One small girl dropped a rag doll. The mother jerked her arm hard, hissing correction. The doll lay forgotten in dust.

A sign.

Several townsfolk noticed. Pretended not to.

Elder Bane continued, "We have rented parcels east of here. Temporary dwellings while we... evaluate."

Evaluate was not supposed to sound like judge. But it did.

"We heard," he added, voice silk-thin and loaded, "that six wealthy men dwell nearby. Men of honor, land, and cattle. Godly men who desire wives devoted and gentle. Women who bake, serve, birth, and bow."

Bow.

Pastor Hale felt his spine stiffen.

"They will find," Bane said, "our daughters most... suitable."

An uncomfortable hush settled. Mrs. Hale's hand crept to her cross necklace, thumb rubbing wood. Young Miss Lottie Hale's face paled; she glanced toward the horizon, toward the six ranches, sympathy softening her eyes.

Elder Bane saw everything.

But smiled instead.

A shepherd smile over wolves.

Town chatter circled like restless wind as the Fellowship set up camp eastward, raising tents with rigid discipline. They sang hymns with perfect tone but **no breath of joy**. They cooked skillfully, quietly. They prayed long.

Yet their eyes—too sharp.

Their greetings—too measured.

Their order—too absolute.

Whispers began almost at once.

"Didn't they leave Kansas sudden?"

"Heard there was trouble."

"Pressured neighbors to sell..."

"...at pennies on the acre..."

"...a whole settlement run out by night."

The children of Providence watched wide-eyed from behind fences as the Fellowship drilled obedience in theirs like cattle driven into alignment. Not teaching—**forcing**.

They practiced curtsies by command.

Bowed heads by whistle.

Smiled on cue then dropped it like a shutter.

Whatever this group believed, it was trained, not lived. Holy clothing over hollow bones.

Every evening the Fellowship daughters walked to the highest ridge and gazed westward toward the ranch lands.

Waiting.

Plotting.

Rehearsing meekness like a costume that didn't fit.

They whispered to one another when fathers were not near:

"Soon those men will marry us."

"We shall have land."

"They say cattle worth thousands graze there."

"We will be ranch mistresses."

One girl, older, more tired, asked, "And after marriage?"

A colder voice answered quietly:

"Our men will manage the ranches. They shall be ours."

Another girl swallowed. "But what of those six? They are decent men, they say."

A whisper like a knife:

"Decency is weakness to be shaped."

Yet even among them, **one girl wept at night**, praying God show her a different life. But she did not speak. Fear stitched her silence.

Meanwhile, on their ranch ridge at twilight, six Rangers leaned on railings, unaware wolves in bonnets had pitched tents near their borders.

Marshal rubbed tired eyes. "Feels like a season turnin'. Sky look different."

Boone shrugged. "Spring comin' early maybe."

Hank whispered a nightly prayer over land and cattle.

Carter read a psalm softly.

Thomas stared toward town, heart unsettled for reasons

unknown.

Benn wondered aloud if God had forgotten marriage entirely.

None felt peace.

The ground held breath.

Far away, six beloved women finished packing trunks for the journey home. They did not yet know **God had sent them back to be a shield**.

The Lord often places His daughters ahead of danger, not behind it.

They would walk into a valley where schemers waited—men and women alike—but they would not walk alone.

Providence needed light again.

And the Rangers?

They needed discernment, maturity, and truth.

Heaven was preparing to expose darkness masquerading as piety.

The devil could dress obedience in bonnet and apron.

But God sees every counterfeit lace thread.

The Mercy Six packed without fear, whispering prayers over each other's trunks.

"Lord, guide us."

"Strengthen us."

"Guard our hearts."

"Let us not be deceived."

Naomi whispered Psalm 37:

"Fret not thyself because of evildoers."

Ellie added softly:

"The Lord shall bring forth thy righteousness as the light."

And Lillian breathed:

"Turn away from evil, and do good."

God was turning His daughters toward battle ground disguised as prairie.

Not to lose.

But to reveal.

Because love without discernment is fragile.
And calling without courage is incomplete.

Providence slept under a brewing storm.
The counterfeit wives waited.
The real ones rode soon.

Heaven whispered over every mile and hill:

Truth is coming.

CHAPTER TWELVE — THE STIRRING OF SPIRITS

Winter melted from Missouri like a coat dropped after long burden. The earth softened. The creek began to whisper again instead of groan beneath ice. The first green threads of hope pushed from soil.

Providence breathed in spring.

But something else breathed with it.

At first, it was only a feeling—a prickle along the pastor's spine one evening as he carried wood into the parsonage. His wife fussed with stew pots and stopped suddenly, spoon hovering, as though hearing a sound no one else did.

She whispered, "I smell deceit."

He looked at her, startled. "We know nothing yet."

"I smell deceit," she repeated softly. "And the Spirit does not lie."

Across town, Mrs. Kepper at the mercantile dropped a tin lid. It clanged. She pressed a hand to her chest. "Lord, hedge us in."

She could not explain why.

Schoolchildren who usually skipped home felt suddenly quiet, glancing at the ridge where the Submit & Serve Fellowship camped. Parents began calling little ones inside earlier than usual.

At dusk, when lanterns glowed warm behind window glass, shadows stretched longer than they should. And the wind, once playful around the church steeple, hushed as if listening.

Providence did not yet know wickedness wore bonnets nearby, but souls felt trouble before eyes saw it.

Meanwhile, at the Ranch

The six Rangers remained at work as though the world still lay simple. Winter calves bawled, fence posts needed mending, horses needed shoeing. Ranch life never paused for emotion nor curiosity—it marched by chores and seasons.

Hank sang hymns softly as he brushed his gelding, unaware danger prayed his name elsewhere. Boone practiced speaking courteously to imaginary ladies again in the barn, unaware counterfeit gentleness practiced curtsies on their hill. Thomas read a psalm before bed each night, unaware someone prayed to take what was his.

Marshal, always the most spiritually sensitive, paused one morning while saddling his horse. The sky felt strange. Heavy. Watching.

He frowned faintly. "Something's comin'."

Carter threw hay into troughs. "Storm?"

"Not the kind you see."

Benn paused mid-hitching. "You feel somethin'?"

Marshal hesitated. "Like the ground's holdin' its breath."

They shrugged off his thought. Men busy with labor rarely sense wolves in silence.

But angels nearby sharpened swords in the unseen realm.

The Fellowship Begins to Unmask

On the rented parcels, things changed. Still quiet, but sharpened quiet.

Elder Bane stood one morning giving orders, voice like a knife hidden in velvet.

"Girls, rehearse again."

A line of daughters bowed their heads. Spoke their rehearsed lines:

"Yes, husband."

"I obey gladly."

"Your will leads my joy."

"I do not think; I trust."

A few townsfolk journeyed near to deliver supplies. They watched. Their stomachs tightened.

Brother Whitlock whispered to his wife, "That ain't devotion. That's bondage."

She replied softly, "And God don't order chains for women, only coverings."

One young Fellowship girl, hair thick and dark as walnut wood, stole a glance toward them. Just a glance. Her eyes flickered with longing, rebellion, confusion—a spark that had not yet been stamped out.

Her mother seized her wrist hard. "Eyes down."

The poor child obeyed. But inside, something trembled.

Seed God had planted long before that group claimed her.

Town Women Begin to Discern

Mrs. Hale invited a few Fellowship women to help sew quilts for a new baby in town. The visitors stitched perfectly—but never laughed, never told stories, never relaxed their shoulders.

They spoke of marriage like obligation.

Children like duty.

Joy like sin.

Mrs. Hale asked gently, "Do you not ever bake for pleasure?"

One answered:

"Pleasure is flesh. Duty glorifies."

Mrs. Hale smiled politely, though a chill ran over her arms. "The Lord Himself rested and delighted."

They blinked.

They did not understand rest.

Later, as the Fellowship wives left, Mrs. Hale whispered to the pastor, "These women live like lambs in a pen. But I sense wolves behind the gate."

The pastor nodded. "We watch. We pray."

And night fell quiet as a held breath.

Word Travels in Whisper Form

Mrs. Kepper's niece, a young woman who once lived near Kansas Territory, arrived unexpectedly for visit. When she heard where the Submit & Serve Fellowship had resettled, her face drained of color.

"Aunt," she whispered, "I know them."

"You do?"

"They masquerade as saints. But they buy up land by threat, not bargain. They forced widows to sell. Drove one family from their home by lies. They were chased out by torches one night."

Mrs. Kepper's voice was low. "Are you certain?"

"As certain as I am breathing."

"Should we warn—"

"We wait. We pray. Truth exposes itself when pressed by holiness."

Mrs. Kepper shivered. She felt suddenly grateful the Rangers lived disciplined, sober lives—they had discernment, honor. Surely God would shield them.

Yet her heart whispered, almost trembling:

Lord, hurry. Bring back the ones who see deeper

The Rangers Still Unaware

On the ranch, super bowls scraped empty. Candlelight flickered on wood walls. The men sat tired and content in a circle near the fire.

Boone leaned back, sighing. "Town's been quiet lately."

Hank chuckled. "Quiet's a blessin'. Means no foolishness."

Marshal stared at the flames. "Sometimes quiet is warning dressed in peace."

Carter looked at him, eyebrow raised. "You frettin' like a hen with fox dreams."

Marshal shook his head slow. "Just listenin' to my spirit."

Thomas nodded. "He ain't wrong. The Lord stirs a man before things shift."

Benn smirked softly. "Lord stirred us long enough. Maybe somethin' good comin'."

They grinned, unaware danger wore skirts, not guns.

Unaware God was stirring because **their true help was riding toward them**.

On the Road — The Mercy Six

Meanwhile, far east, trunks were loaded again. A stagecoach waited. Six bonnets tied under six firm chins. The Mercy Six stood outside the college gates, each woman laying a hand on the wrought iron like saying farewell to a chapter.

Students gathered and cried softly.
Teachers hugged them, blessed them.
The dean prayed over them.

Ellie lifted her eyes to the mountains.
"Lord, go before us."

Maggie whispered, "Give us courage."

Naomi clutched her Bible. "Guide our feet."

Ruth Ann exhaled slowly. "Shield our hearts."

Josie spoke soft, "Prepare what waits."

Lillian closed her eyes. "And prepare us to see without flinching."
They boarded.
The coach lurched.

Hooves struck earth.
And the long journey west began again.

Not running to men.
Returning to destiny.

Between Pennsylvania and Missouri lay miles of forest, river, and prairie. But also **time for hearts to ask God for sight sharper than longing**.

Even at rest stops, they saw signs.
A wagon woman nursing bruises behind a smile forced.
A preacher with too much command and not enough humility.
A mother hushed too sharply, not for safety but control.

And each sight confirmed:
Women were not created to bow to men.
Women bow only to God.

Submission in Christ is shared reverence.
Forced obedience is devil's work in Sunday clothes.

They prayed deeper each night.

Lord, let us not be caught unaware.
Lord, give us courage to confront wrong.
Lord, let Your daughters be lioness when needed.

Wind carried their whispers across the miles.

Back in Providence — Something Breaks Open

Three weeks before the Mercy Six would arrive, a Fellowship daughter broke.

During a quilting circle at the church hall, one young woman— Hannah Bane, the elder's niece—dropped her needle, burst into tears, and blurted:

"I do not want to marry a man I never met! I do not want to pretend joy I do not feel! I want to choose love, not duty!"

Her mother gasped.

Her aunt hissed her name.

Her father's face burned with fury.

But Mrs. Hale, swift as Holy Spirit wind, stepped forward and gathered the girl into her arms.

"Hush, child. You may speak here."

The Fellowship wives froze, horrified—not by pain but by disobedience.

A crack had formed in their armor.

Pastor Hale's eyes softened. "Truth has a sound. And that is it."

One of the men from the Fellowship lunged to drag Hannah away, but Deacon Elmore stepped between them, jaw set.

"Touch her in anger, you answer to God first and us second."

A storm broke then—not of fists, but of eyes opening.

Providence women looked at Fellowship women and saw chains. Providence men looked at Fellowship men and saw wolves.

A current shifted.

Heaven moved.

Hell trembled.

Something wicked had been named.

God had begun exposing the impostors.

And far to the east, the Mercy Six sat in a hotel on their travel route, unaware a child had cried for help in their name.

But the Holy Spirit whispered to Ellie as she prayed that night:

A snare has been set for the righteous.

Return to break it.

She opened her eyes slowly.

Then she smiled—not with excitement, but with **holy resolve**.

"We are needed," she told the others softly.

And the prairie wind carried her whisper west—
"God goes before us."

CHAPTER THIRTEEN — THE HOMECOMING GOD ARRANGED

The train whistle cried long through Missouri hills, rolling across pasture and timber, stirring dust on quiet roads, shaking windows in Providence just before dawn as it pulled into the station.

Sleepy travelers yawned. A conductor shouted final calls. But the train held a different hush, a sacred hush — as though angels traveled with it.

Inside one of the private passenger cars sat six women, dressed in refined traveling dresses — deep blues, warm olives, and soft creams. Bonnets neat, gloves clean, backs straight, expressions anchored in quiet certainty.

They had left in tears once.

But they returned as **teachers, builders, and covenant daughters**, not broken hearts searching for what once stung.

Ellie lifted her gaze as the train hissed to a halt.
"This time," she whispered,
"We step forward, not back."

Naomi nodded, smoothing her skirt.
"We are not returning to be chosen,
but to continue choosing God."

Maggie breathed deep, smelling home soil through the window.
"Lord walk before us."

Ruth Ann swallowed softly but held steady.
"I feel the air different."

Josie smiled faint, courage flickering like morning flame.
"Yes. Something... expectant."

Lillian pressed her gloved hand over her heart.
"Let it be unto us as He wills."

The train door opened.
Feet touched wood steps.
They descended with grace — not looking for faces, not shrinking from looks — women who had been carved stronger in absence.

Waiting at the platform were two fine carriages and wagons — polished, crested with Mr. Alderton's seal. The drivers, in neat uniforms, tipped hats respectfully when the ladies approached.

"Miss Mercy Ladies?" the lead driver called gently.

"Yes," Ellie answered, smile polite, posture serene.

"Your residence is prepared, ma'am. A full house, kitchen stocked, linens laid, staff present. Mr. Alderton said you were not to want for comfort nor safety."

Comfort.
Safety.
Two things they had prayed for on long Pennsylvania nights.

They exchanged soft glances — humbled, grateful, but still braced.

They climbed into the carriages — no town parade, no public attention. Their return was not spectacle, but **assignment**.

The wheels began rolling toward the new homestead site — east valley, gentle slope, wildflowers waving in April wind. The house rose white against green, windows shining like hope.

It did not shout. It welcomed.

And they entered not as visitors — but as leaders.

Servants curtsied, took trunks inside, offered warm bread and tea. There were polished floors, two parlors, a study, a sewing room, guest quarters, and a chapel nook near a sunlit window.

Naomi whispered, "God prepared a table before us."

Lillian touched a carved wooden bannister. "It's lovely."

Ruth Ann breathed, relief and purpose mingling. "We are settled by His hand."

Josie ran fingers over a linen cloth. "Providence indeed."

Maggie peeked into the kitchen and smiled — fresh herbs, flour barrels, polished copper pots. "I feel a hymn risin'."

Ellie stood in the parlor window overlooking distant ridges, voice soft but resolute:

"We do not chase men.
We build God's work.
And if love finds us again,
it will meet us here — on purpose."

They unpacked slowly that day, each woman taking her time, praying over drawers and rooms, asking covering, blessing, discernment.

In town, word trickled like spring creek.

"The Mercy ladies? Back?"
"Arrived by train, did you hear?"
"Living out east — sponsor bought a house!"
"Bless the Lord, they came home educated and whole."

Some whispered joy.
Some whispered worry.
Some whispered prophecy.

The Submit & Serve Fellowship felt a shift in wind — a disturbance to their plan — though they did not yet know its shape.

Fathers watched the ridge with narrowing eyes.
Mothers tightened grips on daughters' arms.
Daughters stole glances at the horizon, where real strength moved like early dawn behind lace curtains.
A power they could not mimic had returned.

Not noise.
Not competition.
Holiness.

God's daughters had stepping feet again in Missouri soil, and darkness shivered.

Meanwhile, on the Ranger land — five miles out — six men worked fence and drove calves.

They didn't know why the air felt different.
They didn't know why their hearts beat faster that morning, restless, unsettled.

Marshal paused mid-saddle tightening.
"Feels like somethin' near."

Hank nodded slow.
"Like somethin' good comin' over a hill."

Thomas murmured, "Or someone."

Carter turned toward the distant road.
"I don't see anything."

Boone shrugged, but softly.
"Sometimes you don't see the change. You feel it first."

Benn stared toward town, unaware eyes were already searching for six faces he carried unspoken in prayer.

The morning wind lifted dust and carried the faintest echo of women's voices setting teacups on polished wood, the rustle of skirts across hardwood, and a hymn drifting up stairwells in a rented house that felt like promise.

The Mercy Six had come back, not to be chosen —
but to stand, to teach, to build, to protect, to **witness God unfold justice and love in His time**.

The land stirred.
Heaven leaned in.
Evil listened and counted its days.

And Providence felt it —

the real wives had returned,

and the counterfeit ones would soon tremble.

CHAPTER FOURTEEN — QUIET THUNDER RETURNS

They did not march back into Providence with trumpets.
They did not call for attention.
They came like God's weather — silent, sure, and full of purpose.

In their rented home on the hill, the Mercy Six sat around their dining table each morning, tea poured steaming, notebooks spread neat as scripture pages, skirts brushing polished chairs. The table was covered in architectural drawings, curriculum outlines, stove supply lists, student room arrangements, budget ledgers, sewing patterns, and scripture verses they believed would undergird a generation of young women.

Ellie spoke first as always, posture straight, voice steady.
"We build what the Lord commands. Let our hearts stay fixed."

Naomi read from Psalm 127 softly, voice a gentle bell:
"Except the Lord build the house, they labour in vain that build it."

A whisper of agreement passed around the table like a prayer shawl.

Ruth Ann reviewed financial estimates with sober precision.
Josie sorted through correspondence from families applying to send daughters.
Lillian organized domestic sciences schedules.
Maggie sketched a kitchen blueprint, hand steady, heart steady.

They moved with quiet dignity.

Not avoiding town — simply living above its noise.

When the mayor and sheriff arrived two days after their return, hats respectfully in hand, boots wiped before stepping through the door, they found the Mercy Six already deep in purpose.

Mayor Whitcomb cleared his throat softly.

"Ladies, Providence is mighty honored God turned your steps this way again."

Ellie offered a small, gracious nod.

"We are grateful for the town's welcome. The Lord led us, and so we came."

Sheriff Porter looked around the bright parlor, seeing the warmth of sunrise against lace curtains, stacks of ledgers, textbooks, a globe, scripture cards pinned near the mantel.

"You've wasted no time."

Ruth Ann smiled, gentle but proud.

"Idle hands are not our calling."

The mayor sat only when invited, his voice warm.

"The school land is surveyed. Folks are already offerin' materials. Providence has waited for a place to shape our daughters into strong Christian women."

Maggie's eyes softened.

"We believe in shaping daughters who think, speak, and serve boldly — not silently."

Sheriff grinned a little.

"Well I reckon we need strength more than quiet, these days."

The mayor chuckled low.

"And wisdom more than show."

Josie asked calmly, "Town reception?"

The sheriff leaned forward.

"They are thrilled. Might not say it real loud yet, but folks... they prayed y'all back. You don't know what your absence showed this place."

Lillian folded her hands, voice soft.

"And your town prayed faithfully while we were gone. We felt it."

There was quiet then — not awkward, but reverent. The kind that fills a room where God sits, listening.

Across the valley, the Submit & Serve Fellowship heard whispers too.

Late afternoon sunlight slanted through their tents when a boy from town rode by delivering flour.

"They're back," he announced innocently.

"The Mercy girls. College teachers. They stay in that house on the hill."

Silence fell like frost.

The eldest daughters froze mid-stitch.

Mothers stiffened.

Fathers exchanged looks sharp as flint striking stone.

One woman whispered, breath tight, "Them?"

A young daughter murmured, "Are they beautiful?"

Another answered bitterly, "They have *presence.* Worse than beauty."

Elder Bane's mouth tightened.

"They were supposed to stay gone."

His wife bowed her head in false piety.

"It is a test of obedience, surely. The devil returns with charm."

Charity Bane, his eldest daughter, lifted her eyes ever so slightly.

"Perhaps we are meant to… compete."

Her voice trembled — whether in fear or ambition none could say.

Another whispered, "Men like those Rangers would choose condition of heart, not quiet tongue alone."

A harsh hiss followed.

"We trained for docility. For wives' crowns. We will not be

pushed out."

Envy, sharp as thorn, coiled among them.

Fear crouched too — jealousy braided with greed.

And wickedness does not love to be challenged by righteousness.

In town, whispers spread like thin smoke.

"The Mercy ladies are home!"

"They renting that house east. Fine place. Sponsored."

"They look refined. Graceful."

"They came back changed."

"No — they came back *grown.*"

Some voices held joy.

Some held awe.

One or two held resentment — especially from households who preferred women quiet and unseen. Even righteousness has enemies.

Mothers cleaning porches paused to watch the house hillward when sun hit the windows just right. Girls walked home from school imagining themselves someday inside those lessons, learning bread and scripture, dignity and strength.

And a strange hush followed:

Hope does that to a town.

Two days later, in a dry-goods shop, a ranch hand burst through the door, breathless from riding post.

"Hear this— they're back!"

The store went still.

Back near the flour barrels, where the Rangers sometimes purchased supplies, young Jesse Wheeler's eyes widened. He didn't say names. He didn't need to.

Rangers.

Mercy ladies.

All anyone ever whispered.

He raced his horse down the road toward the ranch.

That evening, near sunset, six tired cowboys gathered at the corral, brushing sweat-damp horses, dust heavy on their boots.

Jesse rode in fast, too fast — spooking a mare.

Boone straightened, jaw set.
"Boy, what's your hurry?"

Jesse was panting.
"They're back."

Marshal's brush stopped mid-stroke.
"Who's back?"

Jesse swallowed, wide-eyed.
"Those college ladies. The ones you... well... the ones from before."

Silence.

Breath left lungs.
Boots stilled in dirt.
Hearts kicked hard beneath shirt buttons.

Thomas went still as fence post.
Boone looked away sharp, jaw tightening.
Hank's knees felt weak enough to bend.
Benn swallowed pride and fear both.

Carter's voice cracked quiet.
"Where?"

"Up east hill. In a big house. Sponsor sent it. They here to build a school."

A moment passed — long, heavy, holy.

Marshal closed his eyes once, slow.
Like a man praying without words.
Then he said low:

"God sent 'em back."

Boone didn't turn, but his voice broke.
"We ain't ready."

Thomas murmured, "We better get ready."

Hank brushed the horse again, hand shaking just slightly.
"We wronged them by silence."

Benn whispered, no sarcasm left in him,
"We wronged ourselves worse."

None spoke of riding to see them.
None dared hope yet.

Men can face cattle stampedes with less fear than an honest woman's eyes.

Back in their house, lamps glowed warm. The Mercy Six sat on cushioned chairs finishing evening devotions.

Maggie whispered, "I felt a stirring in the air today."

Naomi nodded. "Spirit jolted me twice."

Ruth Ann closed her ledger softly.
"Town hearts tremble."

Josie looked toward the window where moonlight traced curtains.
"Something coming."

Lillian's voice barely above a hum,
"Something testing."

Ellie lifted her Bible.
"We stay still. We stay hidden in Him. We do not go near what God has not called us near yet."

Amen moved around the room.

They prayed — not for love. Not yet.
For clarity. Courage. Protection.

For Missouri.

Because they could feel it now:
a storm of envy brewing on one hill,
a storm of longing stirring on another,
and in between them — six women chosen to walk steady where hearts clashed and schemes brewed.

Quiet as dawn, powerful as thunder that waits.

They were back.
Not seeking.
Not begging destiny.
But **standing**.

And jealous eyes saw it.

Soon — very soon — these two worlds would collide again.

But not today.

Tonight, belonged to prayer.
To peace.
To women who learned the strength of stillness.

Tomorrow would hold battle.
Tomorrow would hold truth.

And somewhere on a ranch porch, six men sat in the dark, hats tipped low, staring toward the hill where lamps burned warm in windows they remembered.

None spoke.
All felt.

And heaven whispered over Missouri:

Love waits.
Wolves watch.
And only God decides the hour.

CHAPTER FIFTEEN — WOLVES TRY THE GATE

Spring sun stretched warm over Missouri, soft as God's own palm. Prairie grass lifted, green and clean. Calves bawled in pastures. Schoolchildren laughed along the riverbanks. Providence breathed expectation.

For something holy was being prepared on one hill,
while something false crouched low on another.

The Mercy Six spent morning hours in prayer, planning, study. Their parlor often hummed like a hive of purposeful bees — pens scratching, teacups clinking, Bibles open, maps unrolled.

They had returned different women — no longer soft-hearted innocents seeking belonging. Now they were **temples of instruction and discernment**, walking in the quiet authority of women who know obedience costs but yields glory.

They did not go into town recklessly. They chose their steps. They kept private. They protected peace like a jewel.

And Providence watched them with reverence.

Meanwhile, the Submit & Serve Fellowship stirred in envy and urgency.

Elder Marcus Bane paced his tent like a wolf who smelled a shepherd.
"They threaten our plan."
His wife murmured, "We must move quickly."

Their eldest daughter, Charity, lifted her chin. "Father, I can approach the Rangers. I am trained."

Another daughter pressed lips thin. "We prepared for this entire journey. We did not leave home to be overshadowed."

Yet the youngest, Hannah, hugged her arms tight, whispering only where no ear but God's heard:
Lord, let me not become a weapon in my father's hand.

But wolves do not ask lambs if they are willing.

First Attempt at Introduction

The Fellowship marched daughters down to the river path near the Ranger pastures under guise of an afternoon hymn stroll. Parasols opened. Dresses straightened. Eyes lowered in practiced false modesty.

Young Hannah trailed behind, praying under breath to be unseen.

Soon, six Rangers rode nearby — returning from checking water troughs. Dust followed them quiet, like a loyal dog.

Boone spotted the line of bonneted figures and slowed his horse. "Well I'll be. Looks like new neighbors."

Carter blinked. "They marched lookin' like a funeral choir."

Thomas sniffed. "Ain't no joy in them. See it in posture."

Marshal lifted his chin slightly, spiritual senses prickling. "Something ain't right in that camp."

Before they had chance to turn away, Elder Bane stepped from shade of trees with pointed politeness.

"Gentlemen. Greetings in holiness. We are the Submit & Serve Fellowship."

Marshal dismounted out of courtesy — but kept distance.
Boone nodded slow, hat in hand but eyes guarded.
Carter forced a polite smile.
Hank slid down quietly, posture respectful but uneasy.
Thomas and Benn remained mounted, reins tight.

Elder Bane continued, "These are our daughters. Pure. Modest. Trained in obedience and homemaking. Seeking godly husbands who lead."

Charity curtsied slowly, eyes lifted just enough to appear bashful.

The other girls followed, voices in unison:

"We greet you in righteousness."

Only Hannah did not lift her head. Tears trembled at the corner of her lashes—prayer tears, not fear.

Marshal's gaze moved across the daughters — polite, steady — then fixed on Hannah. Something holy stirred in him. The Spirit whispered:

Not all who bow are humble.
Not all who break are weak.

Hank swallowed hard. He felt something too — the difference between a trained lamb and a held captive one.

Boone forced courtesy.

"We thank y'all kindly for your greetin'. But we ain't courtin'."

Elder Bane smiled thin and cold.

"All Christian fellowship begins with acquaintance."

Thomas' jaw tightened.

"We walk by discernment, not convenience."

Benn's voice stayed mild but firm.

"Lord bless y'all. But we already seek direction from Heaven."

Marshal felt the Spirit thicken around them, like an invisible shield.

"The Lord ain't send us wives by parade, sir. He works quieter."

Elder Bane's eyes narrowed — a serpent noticing prey refusing approach.

"Your refusals may grieve angels."

Marshal answered softly, peacefully, without flinch:

"Some refusals keep angels around us."

And with that, he mounted.

A stir of confusion passed through the Fellowship daughters —
some frightened, some insulted, some shaken.

But Hannah's heart leapt.
For someone had seen truth without her speaking a word.

The Rangers rode off, leaving dust and discernment behind.

Elder Bane's voice turned low and dangerous:
"They resist. We persist."

The young women bowed again — except Hannah, who prayed,
Lord, let truth win.

Town Women Warn the Mercy Six

That evening, Mrs. Hale and Mrs. Kepper arrived with covered
baskets. They did not come gossiping. They came protective,
spiritual.

Ellie welcomed them inside with grace.
Naomi poured tea.
Ruth Ann set extra chairs.
Maggie laid warm bread.
Josie lit lamps softer.
Lillian offered gentle smiles.

Mrs. Hale folded her hands.
"Daughters, we need to tell you something."

Mrs. Kepper nodded solemnly.
"Another group has come. Looks devout. Ain't."

Naomi's eyes sharpened.
"We sensed something unclean on the wind."

Mrs. Hale leaned forward, voice low:
"They aim for the Rangers. Trained their girls to act docile. Not
natural. Forced."

Josie's jaw set with holy fire.
"Counterfeit submission."

Ruth Ann nodded.
"Wolves in linen."

Lillian's hands trembled slightly.

"Do the men know?"

"No," Mrs. Kepper answered. "Not truly. They just wary."

Ellie's gaze lifted, peace and resolve entwined.
"We will not interfere. But we will pray and watch."

Mrs. Hale exhaled relief.
"God brought you back for a reason."

Naomi whispered,
"Not to fight flesh and blood —
but to guard the righteous and expose deception."

Mrs. Kepper whispered,
"Thank the Lord you're here."

The School Land Blessing

Three days later, all Providence gathered at the building site. Sun high, breeze warm, choir of meadowlarks overhead. The sheriff stood solemn. Mayor smiling. Town folk holding hymn books. Pastors from three congregations present.

And at the center stood the Mercy Six — plain but radiant, with aprons tied over modest dresses, Bibles held gently at their waists, hair pinned with simple grace. Nothing glittered but their peace.

When they bowed heads to pray, wind lifted soft around them — skirts swaying like wheat, ribbons fluttering, heaven brushing earth.

Ellie prayed aloud:
"Lord, bless this land.
May girls leave here wise and free in You.
Let no false teaching pass these gates.
Let no counterfeit spirit cross this foundation.

Where You reign, deception cannot root."

Naomi added,
"Make this a sanctuary of discernment."

Maggie whispered,
"And a hearth of joy."

Josie declared,
"A place where women are taught strength and sweetness both."

Lillian breathed,
"And where love grows honest, not forced."

Ruth Ann finished,
"And may this ground reject every wolf."

The crowd said "Amen."

A hush fell.
Then a breeze rose — not harsh, but holy — swirling dust into golden light, lifting hymn pages, stirring hair, bowing heads.

Townfolk gasped softly.
Mrs. Hale wept.
Children stared wide-eyed.

Even the pastor felt his knees go weak for a moment.

And far at the edge of the clearing, unseen by most, the Submit & Serve Fellowship watched — stiff, unsettled.
One daughter trembled.
One mother gripped her arm too tight.
Elder Bane scowled at the wind.

Wolves do not like the Shepherd's breath.

Evening — Quiet Confirmation

That night, the Mercy Six knelt at their bedside in the big rented home. Candles flickered. Outside, frogs croaked by the creek. Peace wrapped around them like a shawl.

Ellie whispered,
"The Lord is here."

Naomi nodded, tears soft.
"He stands between us and the snare."

Lillian murmured,
"When wolves see truth, they howl."

Ruth Ann prayed,
"Give the men discernment, Lord."

Josie added,
"And guard our hearts from old wounds."

Maggie whispered, voice trembling,
"And if love returns, let it be Your doing, not our longing."

They rose, and peace sat with them.

At the Ranch — Realization Rising

Marshal stood outside under stars, hat in hand, looking toward the hill where candlelight glowed faint in the Mercy home.

Boone joined him, leaning on the rail.
"Think they know about them schemers?"

Marshal nodded once.
"They see clearer than we ever did."

Thomas approached, voice solemn.
"You reckon we get a second chance?"

Marshal didn't move his gaze.
"If God aims to rewrite hearts, no man can stop it. If He don't, no prayer can force it."

Carter murmured,
"I ain't the man I was. But I ain't yet the man I pray to be."

Hank whispered,
"Lord, don't let counterfeit steal what was meant."

Benn bowed his head.
"God forgive us for bein' blind."

Silence.
Stars bright.
Hearts soft.
Angels watching.

Providence exhaled under moonlight, not knowing a war had

already begun — not of rifles, but of spirits.

And the Mercy Six slept in peace, while the wolves planned through clenched teeth, and the Rangers learned humility night by night.

Heaven smiled.
For nothing was out of God's hand.

Love waited.
Truth sharpened.
Jealousy churned.
Destiny approached.

Now the story turned.

CHAPTER SIXTEEN — A CHANCE NOT PLANNED BY MAN

Hannah Bane had never belonged to the Submit & Serve Fellowship, though she had worn their dresses and bowed her head at their commands since childhood. She had been found wandering a creek bank at three years old, memory soft as butterbrush and voice smaller than a robin's chirp. Elder Bane's wife had taken her in because she could work early and obey quickly.

Twenty years passed, yet Hannah still felt like borrowed linen never meant for their table.

Where the other women learned silence like scripture, she learned silence like survival. Where they lowered eyes in pride of submission, she lowered hers in fear of the world outside camp.

But her heart — it never quieted.

She watched birds dance above treetops and wondered why women could not. She watched creek water sparkle and wondered why laughter was forbidden. When she prayed, she did not sound like the Fellowship; she whispered to God like a girl asking if He remembered where she came from.

She never believed submission was slavery until she saw the Mercy Ladies return. Their modest bonnets and soft manners looked nothing like the Fellowship's frozen obedience. Those women held heads high because their hearts knew liberty, not fear. They bowed to God, not to men.

Hannah watched from a grove on the hill that day, cheeks hot with longing, as the Mercy Six prayed over school ground, wind circling them like an answer. She clutched her torn hymnbook to her chest.

Her heart whispered in awe:
So this is what holiness looks like when not chained.

She pressed her palm over her heart. She could not yet walk their path — but she knew now that it existed.

And when truth is seen, captivity trembles.

Hank on the Ridge

Hank Pratt — 25 years old, second son of a God-fearing Missouri farmer, hired ranch hand on the Rangers' spread — had worked twelve hours that day mending fence line and riding to check water troughs. Hard work suited him like boots suit earth. He hummed low hymns while repairing things, never quick to judge, always quick to pray.

He remembered the Mercy women well — good women, decent, strong but gentle, with smiles soft as sunrise. He had delivered sacks of flour and honey to them while the Rangers trained months ago. And though he never presumed to be noticed by such ladies, he never forgot the peace he felt on their porch.

Hank knew modesty.
Hank knew gentleness.
Hank also knew when something felt wrong in the air.

The Submit & Serve folks unsettled him. He saw their daughters walking stiff, voices too quiet, shoulders too tense. Righteousness bows by choice. Fear bows by command.

Hank prayed for them.

Now, as he finished his ride early evening, leading his horse down a wooded path by the creek, he hummed "Come Thou Fount" under breath.

Streams gurgled over stones. Crickets chirped. His soul settled.

Then he heard soft crying.

A woman crying.

It wasn't loud. It wasn't wailing. It was a compressed heartbreak, like someone trying not to be heard.

Hank froze. "Hello? Someone there?"

Leaves rustled. A figure moved behind willow branches — a young woman in simple calico and bonnet, shaking shoulders, hands pressed to her face.

Hannah.

She gasped and backed up, tripping slightly over a root. She tried to straighten but tears betrayed her discipline.

Hank dismounted slowly, hands open in peace.
"I mean no harm, ma'am."

She swiped hurriedly at her cheeks, eyes lowering instinctively. "I'm sorry. I'm... I'm not— I should not be here."

Hank softened his voice. He recognized her from seeing the Fellowship in town.
"You ain't in danger. You lost?"

She shook her head. "No. Only... only lost inside."

Her voice trembled like a leaf not meant to fall but shaken loose by wind.

Hank didn't crowd her. He leaned lightly against a cedar trunk, hands in pockets, giving her space.

"That happen sometimes," he said softly. "World turns fast. Hearts take time."

Silence.

Then she whispered, "Why do you speak kindly? Most men only speak command."

Hank blinked, startled. "Because the Lord ain't never spoke command to break me. He speaks command to lift me. A man ought to do as His Maker does."

Her breath caught.

Like a girl hearing water after long desert.

He studied her gentle.
"You from that Fellowship?"

She nodded once, head low.

"They treat you right?"

A pause. Then, in a voice fragile and brave at once:
"I do not know what right feels like. But I know what wrong feels like."

Hank swallowed hard, something fierce and protective rising in him.

"You ain't owned," he murmured. "You ain't property. You a daughter of the Highest, whether they say it or not."

Her lips trembled.
"No one... talks like that where I'm from."

"I reckon that's the problem," Hank said softly.

A quiet fell again — not tense, not frightened.
Tender.
Fragile as new leaf.

She raised her eyes slightly — the first time — and Hank saw they were deep hazel, flecked with gold, like autumn sunlight trying to break free.

"What is your name?" he asked gently.

"Hannah," she whispered. "I am twenty-three."

"Hank," he replied, offering a small respectful nod. "Twenty-five. Ranch hand out past the ridge."

She nodded — not as submission, but acknowledgment.

"You should go," she said softly. "They will... look for me."

"I ain't stoppin' you," he said. "But if you ever need real help — the kind from good folk, not controlling ones — you find me or the sheriff or the pastor's wife."

Her throat bobbed withheld tears.
"Why would strangers care?"

Hank looked toward the evening sky, streaked pink and amber.

"Good folk don't help 'cause they know you.
They help 'cause they know God."

A tear slid down her cheek.
She wiped it quickly, frightened of her own emotion.

"I must go," she whispered. "If they see me speaking—"

"I understand," Hank said, stepping back to give her space. "God go with you."

She darted away like a frightened doe, but paused at the tree line. Did not turn, only whispered so faintly he barely heard:

"Thank you... for seeing me."

Then she disappeared.

Hank stared after her long after the woods stilled.

He whispered, almost a prayer:
"Lord... protect that girl."

That Same Hour — The Mercy Six at Prayer

Ellie's head lifted mid-prayer.
"Someone cried tonight."

Naomi paused, sensing it too.
"Not one of ours."

Ruth Ann whispered, "Someone bound."

Josie murmured, "Lord rescue her."

Maggie pressed hands together, feeling Hannah's trembling spirit across distance.
"A girl in fear."

Lillian breathed,
"And a man stood kind."

They prayed over a girl they didn't yet know and a ranch hand who had already stood like a shield.

God knits threads long before human eyes notice the tapestry.

Back at the Fellowship Camp

Hannah slipped in silently. But Elder Bane noticed damp lashes. Red eyes. A different air.

"Where were you."

She lowered her gaze. "By the water. Praying."

"You return changed."

A tremor ran through her spine.
She whispered truth in courage's smallest form:
"Sometimes truth touches us where chains cannot reach."

His eyes sharpened.
"You spoke to someone."

She swallowed. Didn't answer.

He grabbed her wrist, grip strong, voice low and cruel under piety.
"Speak."

Hannah finally lifted her eyes — not in rebellion, but in holy defiance:
"I spoke to kindness."
"And you will not take that from me."

For the first time in her life, she did not bow.

He saw it.
Fear and fury churned behind his calm expression.

That night, Hannah whispered to God,
"If You open a door, I will run through it."

And Heaven whispered back,
Door already opening.

At the Ranch — Campfire Truth

Hank returned late, quieter than usual. The Rangers noticed.

Boone nudged him. "You look like you saw a ghost."

Hank shook his head.
"No ghost. A girl."

They all stilled.

Marshal leaned forward. "From town?"

"No," Hank murmured. "From that sect. The quiet one with sad eyes."

Thomas's jaw clenched.
"Trouble?"

"She ain't trouble. Trouble holding her."

Carter breathed slow.
"That's how captivity looks."

Hank whispered,
"She ain't theirs. I think God tryin' to bring her out."

Boone sighed.
"And when God starts bringin' women out of bondage, you best prepare. Freedom draws battle."

Marshal nodded.
"And angels draw swords."

They bowed heads.
Prayed without words.
Felt destiny shift.

Hannah had tasted kindness.
Hank had seen a captive.
The Mercy Six had prayed her name without knowing it.
The wolves stirred.
The Shepherd moved.
And Missouri held its breath.

The appointed season had arrived.

CHAPTER SEVENTEEN — A DAUGHTER PULLED FROM THE SNARE

Morning broke soft across Missouri hills, dew clinging like pearls to meadow grass. Hank saddled his horse early, breath misting faint in the cool dawn. He could not shake the image of Hannah's trembling voice the night before. The memory tugged at him like a prayer string tied around his ribs.

He whispered to the Lord as he tightened the cinch,
"Give me eyes to see, and heart to obey."

Then he mounted and rode toward the creek again, as though heaven nudged his reins.

Birds trilled. Creek water whispered peace. But a quiet sob broke the morning stillness — the sound of someone trying not to make sound at all.

Hannah sat beneath the willow again, knees drawn up, arms wrapped around herself, face buried. But this time, her sleeves had slipped, and bruises bloomed dark against pale skin — hand-shaped shadows of control.

Hank froze mid-step.

A heat rose through him. Not anger of man, but fire of righteousness — that quiet holy fury of one who sees injustice touch the undefended.

"Miss Hannah," he said gently.

She startled hard, scrambling to hide her arms, but too late. Shame flooded her face.

"I— I must go," she breathed. "You cannot see me like this."

"I already have," Hank answered, voice steady as solid ground. "And I will not stand idle."

Tears spilled despite her trying to swallow them down.

"They will come for me," she whispered. "They always come for what tries to be free."

Hank knelt to her level, but did not touch her. He knew a wounded bird trusted slowly.

"Hannah, listen careful. You are not theirs to return to. You belong to God, not chains."

Her voice broke in a whisper,
"I do not know how to belong to freedom."

"That's why I'm takin' you to women who do."

Her head shot up, eyes wide with both hope and terror.
"No. They will punish me if they find I left."

"Them punishing you is why we go."

She shook her head hard, panic rising,
"They say I am ungrateful when frightened."

Hank's voice softened into a protective tone stronger than any wall,
"They say wrong. And wrong said long enough feels like truth. But it ain't."

He stood, extending his hand but letting her choose.

"Hannah, come with me. The Mercy ladies will shelter you. The sheriff will stand between you and harm. The Lord Himself walks this road."

She stared at his hand, trembling.
Then she whispered,
"I have waited twenty years for someone to speak like that to

me."

Slow as dawn spreading over fields, she placed her hand in his. And Hank felt something holy move — not romance yet, but **calling**, protection, destiny.

He lifted her gently onto his horse and mounted behind, keeping respectful distance so she felt safe. She clutched the saddle horn like it was the last solid thing in her life.

The horse stepped forward, hooves thudding a rhythm of deliverance. Grass bowed under them as though making way for a child God had always planned to rescue.

The Mercy House — A Refuge Prepared

The Mercy Six were in morning prayer when Hank knocked. Ellie rose first, Naomi beside her. When they opened the door and saw Hannah's tear-stained face and bruised arms, no one asked a question.

The Spirit spoke louder than words.

"Come in, dear heart," Ellie said, voice like warm bread breaking.

Hank helped Hannah down. She stumbled, legs weak, but Naomi caught her gently. The women brought her inside, wrapped her in a shawl, and sat her near the hearth. Ruth Ann fetched cool water. Josie whispered psalms. Maggie prepared warm milk and honey. Lillian brought salve and clean cloth.

Hannah shook with sobbing she had held for years.
Ellie laid a gentle hand near — not on — her shoulder.

"Cry, child. Tears water what God is about to grow."

Hannah lifted wet eyes.
"Do you not fear them?"

Naomi answered calmly,
"We fear only failing God."

Ruth Ann spoke gentle firmness,
"No daughter of heaven returns to chains once angels open a gate."

Hannah tried to speak but words broke.
"They said I was found worthless and must earn value."

Lillian shook her head softly.
"No, dear. You were found valuable, and the enemy tried to bury the truth."

Maggie whispered,
"Look at us. God restores women."

Hank stood near the door, hat in hand, voice low.
"She needs protection. And I ain't sendin' her back."

Ellie nodded.
"You did right bringing her."

Naomi looked at Hannah's bruises again and whispered,
"Lord, defend the humble."

Josie placed a Bible in Hannah's hands, not forcing — offering.
"You are seen. You are loved. You are free."

Hannah wept all over again, face in hand.

The Sheriff Arrives

Sheriff Porter came within the hour, alerted by Hank's ride into town. He saw the bruises and his jaw tightened.

"No one touches a woman in my county and calls it righteousness."

Hannah trembled,
"They will demand I return."

"And they will be denied," the sheriff said firmly. "Law protects you. My badge covers you. God witnesses you."

He turned to Ellie.
"She stays with you ladies."

Ellie nodded,
"No harm crosses this threshold. Not by flesh nor spirit."

The Sect Learns

Word spread fast — wolves smell lost sheep.

By afternoon, Elder Bane heard Hannah was missing. Rage simmered under his piety.

"We retrieve what is ours."

His wife hissed agreement.

"Or we lose authority."

And jealousy flared — not only for Hannah, but because rumor spread that the Rangers refused their daughters politely but firmly.

Failure tasted bitter to them.

A council meeting formed under canvas tents that evening.

One voice whispered,

"We cannot lose the Rangers."

Another hissed,

"We cannot lose the girl. She knows too much."

Another,

"They are back — those Mercy teachers. They draw hearts. They threaten us."

Plans sharpened like knives in soft cotton.
Schemes braided.

Tonight, they would not strike — but tomorrow, perhaps.

Church and a Picnic

Sunday sunlight fell over Providence. Church bells rang. The Rangers entered the chapel weary but upright, looking forward to worship, not battle.

But when service ended and they stepped outside, the Submit & Serve daughters encircled them — bonnets low, hands folded, voices dripping docility.

"We have prepared a picnic in your honor," Charity announced with false modesty.

Marshal looked around at the circle — gentle eyes, soft voices — but something predatory beneath.

Boone whispered sideways,

"We outnumbered?"

Carter smirked,
"No, they out-Holy-toned."

Thomas folded arms.
"We'd best walk careful."

Benn shrugged,
"A meal never hurt nobody — but manipulation does."

Hank whispered prayer under his breath.

The Rangers agreed politely, not to encourage — but to understand.

They walked to the meadow by the river, the sect daughters opening baskets like staging a scene. Food plain, smiles rehearsed, eyes watchful.

Charity spoke sweet as syrup,
"We desire godly husbands. We are meek. We do not question. We obey."

The air tightened.
Even bluebirds ceased song.

Marshal cleared his throat.
"A godly wife is not meek by force, but gentle by strength."

Thomas added,
"And she speaks wisdom. Scripture says her tongue holds kindness, not silence."

Carter nodded toward the sky,
"And her husband praises her, not commands her."

Boone stared level,
"And obedience ain't virtue unless freely given."

Hank swallowed, remembering Hannah,
"A woman ain't livestock bein' trained. She a helpmeet, not a servant."

Benn capped it gently,
"And if love ain't mutual, it ain't holy."

The sect daughters forced smiles but cracks showed — cheeks

flushing, fingers tightening on napkins.

Charity tried again, voice brittle,
"We do not debate men."

Marshal replied gently,
"Then you never learned to love one."

A hush fell.

The Rangers bowed heads.

"Let us pray," Marshal said.

And they prayed — quietly, powerfully, calling on heaven to reveal truth, guard innocence, and thwart wickedness in sheep's clothing.

The sect women felt exposed. The men felt clarity.
Heaven pressed down, holy and heavy.

After the amen, the Rangers stood.

"Thank y'all kindly," Boone said.
"But we'll take our leave."

They walked away, hats low, hearts sober.

Behind them, the sect daughters trembled between rage and humiliation. A mother hissed, "We were close."

Elder Bane's wife whispered with venom,
"We will not lose."

Anger tightened jaws. Pride boiled.
Schemes darkened into full hunger.

The wolves were done pretending sheep.

Nightfall

Back at the Mercy house, Hannah slept finally — deeply — safe in a guest room, breathing like a child.

Hank sat on the porch rail in moonlight, hat off, staring toward the stars.

Ellie stepped out quietly.
"She is safe."

Hank nodded, voice low,

"I won't let harm find her."

"You are not alone in that," Ellie said gently. "God sent an army of women ahead of her."

He bowed his head.

"Amen."

In the distance, wolves plotted.
In the valley, daughters prayed.
On the ranch, men sharpened discernment instead of weapons.

And heaven, watching Missouri, whispered,

The battle lines are drawn.
Not for war, but for deliverance.

Tomorrow, the wolves would come closer.
But tonight, peace slept in the room down the hall —
and a man on the porch kept quiet vigil,
and six women prayed inside like saints with armor.

God was not absent.
He was preparing victory.

CHAPTER EIGHTEEN — THE SNARE THAT FAILED

The next morning, dawn came gold and clean across the prairie, painting fence rails and barn roofs with heaven's warmth. Cattle lowed, horses stamped, and a wind rustled the pasture grass like prayer fingers.

At the Ranger ranch, the men gathered by the pump well before chores — hats off, heads bowed. They prayed the way working men pray — steady, sincere, words like stones from a riverbed:

"Lord, guard our steps."
"Make us upright."
"Blind us to temptation; sharpen us to danger."
"Keep our hearts clean and our hands blameless."

Marshal added softly,
"And what is hidden… bring to light."

They lifted their heads with peace resting across shoulders like well-worn coats.

Not five miles away, in the sect encampment, another plan brewed — but not from heaven.

Elder Bane's voice was low, sharp as a blade masked in scripture. "The men did not bend. So we push. Quietly. Carefully. We corner one alone. Appear distressed. Cry violation. Gain sympathy. Force marriage or shame."

Gasps sounded from younger girls.

One whispered, trembling,
"That is sin."

Her mother silenced her with a grip on her wrist.

Hannah was gone. Their control frayed. Pride boiled. Jealousy burned. They would not lose the Rangers too.

Three chosen daughters practiced trembling voices, fake tears, fragile posture — wickedness wearing lace.

They waited along a split-rail fence near town road, hiding behind shrub and scripture-painted fans, rehearsing victimhood like venom.

But they did not know God had already moved.

Three Rangers approached together — Boone, Carter, and Thomas — not because they suspected trap, but because they had prayed for wisdom and refused to walk in prideful independence.

One girl stepped out.
Lips trembling, tears feigned, voice soft as deceit can feign,
"Sir... please help me. I... I am frightened and alone."

Another appeared too soon behind her. A third behind her shoulder.

Carter narrowed his eyes.
"Ladies, y'all together. Nobody here alone."

Thomas tipped his hat gently but firmly, stepping back.
"You best go home. Ain't safe for young women lurkin' on country road whisperin' fear."

Boone glanced at tree line — instinct razor sharp.
"We ain't foolish. This ain't a holy setup."

Another girl tried, breathy and dramatic,
"Please, I am in distress—"

Boone lifted a hand gently but stern.
"If a woman truly hurt, she runs to town women, not hides in bushes springin' like quail."

Thomas added,

"And she don't bring audience."

Carter bowed his head, pity under his firmness.

"A wounded lamb bleats. A wolf rehearses."

The sect daughters froze. Their plan exposed before it began.

The three men touched their hat brims and walked on — not boastful, not mocking, simply righteous and covered by prayer.

Behind them, the daughters' faces hardened — not innocent sadness, but thwarted ambition.

Wolves grow hungriest when denied.

Sect tries to reclaim Hannah

Before noon, Elder Bane marched to the sheriff's office, hat stiff, eyes burning with false righteousness.

"My daughter has been stolen."

Sheriff Porter didn't stand. Didn't fidget. He leaned back, thumb resting on his badge, Bible open on his desk.

"Your daughter?"

His tone was soft steel.

"She was under our authority. She belongs to us."

Sheriff's eyes sharpened.

"She belongs to God. She has bruises. She stays where she safe."

Elder Bane's lips thinned.

"This town will regret siding with rebellion."

Sheriff stood now — full height, authority settled deep.

"Sir, if you lay a hand on her again or try to take her by force, you will regret under the law."

Their gazes locked.

Righteous authority does not shout — it stands.

Elder Bane left in silence but fire in his eyes.

The Mercy Six tend to Hannah

At the Mercy house, Hannah sat wrapped in a crochet shawl,

sipping broth.

Her bruises faintly purple, but her eyes brighter already — timid hope blooming.

Ellie read softly from Isaiah:

"He has sent Me to bind up the brokenhearted,
to proclaim liberty to captives…"

Hannah whispered,
"I never knew scripture could hold me gently."

Naomi stroked her hair.
"Scripture is balm, not chain."

Ruth Ann taught her how to breathe steady.
Josie taught her to lift her chin softly.
Maggie braided her hair loose like a free woman.
Lillian read psalms over her like medicine.

And Hannah whispered again and again,
"I am not theirs."

Each time, it sounded stronger.
Each time, the old prison cracked.

Rangers pledge protection

Hank returned that afternoon. Behind him rode Marshal, Boone, and Carter. Hats in hand, eyes solemn, they stood on the porch.

Marshal spoke quiet:
"We heard she's here."

Ellie nodded.
"She is safe."

Boone cleared his throat.
"We ain't men to meddle nor gossip… but she came from darkness. We stand ready."

Carter added,
"No harm come near her without passin' us."

Naomi smiled soft,
"God built her defenders before she cried aloud."

The men bowed heads.

Hank whispered,
"Lord keep her."

They left quietly — no show, only duty.

The sect's desperation turns dangerous

That night, lanterns burned late in the Fellowship camp. Desperation thickened the air. Mothers whispered, men clenched fists, false prayers sounded more like demands.

"We strike soon."
"We take back ours."
"We will not be shamed."

They lit no fire — secret plans prefer darkness.

Hannah's name hissed like flame meeting oil.

But a holy host encamped around her that night.
And dreams stirred on both hills.

God stirs the soil for battle and blessing

At the ranch, Marshal dreamed of a lioness — golden, fierce, standing between lambs and wolves, teeth bared not in savagery but in divine authority.

He woke sweating, whispering,
"Lord, show us women's strength rightly."

At the Mercy house, Hannah dreamed of a gate breaking and a hand reaching, pulling her through into light.

She woke with Maggie holding her, whispering,
"You are delivered."

And across the meadow, in the sect tents, daughters slept with clenched fists and jealous hearts, mothers whispered lies as lullabies, and men plotted in darkness — but none rested.

The devil does not sleep when freedom rises
and God does not sleep while protecting His daughters.

And Providence knew —
before romance could rise,

war would test every heart.

Love would not come easy.
But love ordained never falls late.

CHAPTER NINETEEN — WHEN HEAVEN STANDS GUARD

Hannah woke in the Mercy house that morning to the sound of hymn humming downstairs — a tender tune, slow and soothed, like sunlight filtering through lace curtains. She blinked into new day, not sure yet if she was free or dreaming freedom.

Her sleeve slipped as she rose, and her fingers brushed the fading bruise. It no longer felt like shame. It felt like testimony.

She touched her cheek, whispering,
"Lord... let me never forget You brought me out."

Downstairs, Ellie stood over an open Bible, lips moving silently in prayer. Naomi stirred oats in the morning pot. Ruth Ann set the tea. Maggie trimmed flowers for table vases. Josie checked a small letters pile. Lillian ironed fresh linens for the guest rooms.

Home.

Not blood-home, but spirit-home.

When Hannah descended, six women turned and smiled — a welcome soft as sunrise.

"Good morning, dear heart," Ellie said.

"Rest well?" Naomi asked.

"Your eyes look less frightened," Lillian added warmly.

Hannah swallowed hard, tears forming.

"I rested like a little child."

Naomi squeezed her hand gently.

"You are one."

Hannah's voice cracked.
"I think... I am beginning to believe it."

Before breakfast, a knock sounded.

Sheriff Porter and Pastor Hale stood on the porch, hats respectfully in hand. The Mercy Six invited them in and served tea at the dining table.

Protection Plans & Holy Resolve

Pastor Hale cleared his throat.
"I came to pray with y'all. Word runs deep today."

Sheriff nodded.
"And to set law in order. There may be trouble."

Ellie folded her hands calmly.
"We stand ready."

Pastor opened his Bible.
"When the Lord brings a soul out of bondage, the devil howls. But he howls because his leash is yanked."

Naomi whispered,
"And Heaven does not loosen."

"You will not face this alone," the pastor assured.

Sheriff Porter added, voice low and steady,
"This house is watched. Day and night. Quiet. Respectful. Firm."

Hannah's eyes widened in shock.
"You would do that for me?"

Sheriff smiled softly.
"No ma'am, not just for you. For righteousness."

Pastor Hale prayed with them — not loud, not wild, but with deep authority:

"Lord, place angels round these women.
Let no manipulating tongue prosper.
Expose deceit.
Turn every snare into open shame.
And strengthen the men who stand for truth."

Hannah trembled — not from fear, but from the weight of being defended. Something cracked inside, not breaking — opening.

Revival in Town

That evening, Providence gathered for Wednesday service. The Mercy Six attended quietly, Hannah seated between Naomi and Lillian. Whispers rustled through pews — curiosity, awe, protection.

Pastor Hale stepped to the pulpit and read softly:

"Where the Spirit of the Lord is, there is liberty."

Before he could speak further, a trembling young voice rose from the back — Mrs. Wheeler, tears on her cheeks.

"I feel the Lord stirrin' freedom."

A murmur rolled through the sanctuary — not confusion, but deep Amen stirring.

Another woman stood.

"God is uncoverin' wolves in our midst."

The air thickened with holy electricity — not chaos, but truth piercing veil.

Then a man stood — Deacon Elmore — voice solemn.

"We been fooled by quiet piety. True holiness ain't silent — it's righteous."

Pastor Hale lifted both hands.

"Let the Shepherd expose every thief."

And a trembling overtook the room — chairs creaked under bent knees, tears pooled, hands lifted — not dramatic, but real. Like wheat bending under God's passing wind.

Hannah sobbed silently — not in shame but in healing — and Naomi wrapped an arm around her shoulders.

The Spirit moved like fire passing over wheat but burning only weeds.

One sect woman fled the church before prayer finished — unable to sit under truth's weight.

The Rangers See Hannah Healing

The next morning, Hank came with Marshal and Boone to deliver a note from Carter about a town meeting. They lingered on the porch a respectful distance. Ellie invited them in only when Hannah herself stepped forward shyly and whispered,

"I want to thank him."

Hank removed his hat as she entered the room — and his breath caught just a second.

She stood different now — not bold, but less bent, as though her spine had learned its own worth overnight. Maggie had braided her hair soft and loose; Josie had given her a pale blue shawl. Healing had touched her posture.

Hank's voice was gentle.
"You look safe."

Hannah blushed.
"I am learning."

Boone swallowed and tipped his hat.
"Ma'am, we pray for your strength."

Marshal nodded.
"And your future ain't theirs to decide. Nor ours. It's God's."

Hannah's eyes filled again.
"Thank you. For… standing as men should."

Marshal bowed his head slightly.
"We stand because God sees."

Lillian appeared with warm biscuits, and Hank's stomach growled betraying him.
Hannah laughed — a small, startled sound like a songbird testing wings.

Everyone froze a moment, shocked by the beauty of it.

Hank blinked slowly.
"Well I reckon that's the finest sound this place heard."

Hannah blushed so scarlet she had to turn away.

Josie whispered to Lillian behind her hand,
"Careful, we may have our first miracle romance."

Lillian whispered back,
"Let the Lord do it proper."

Holy Pressure Builds

Word spread across Providence:
"They tried to trap the Rangers."
"The men walked righteous."
"Hannah fled the wolves."
"The Mercy girls shelter her."

The town circled like a flock protecting chick and hen.
Eyes sharpened.
Backs straightened.

The sect felt it like heat.

Their men clenched jaws.
Their women seethed behind prayer shawls.
Daughters quivered — some in fear, some in rage, one or two in envy of freedom.

They whispered dark together in tents:
"We will not lose."

But darkness shook — because heaven had already answered.

The Attempt and God's Shield

That night, when moon hung like silver promise, two sect men crept toward the Mercy house, thinking shadows would hide sin from heaven.

But a lantern flared at Pastor Hale's porch.
A rifle clicked safe in Sheriff Porter's hands.
Two town men stepped from brush — farmers, but fierce.
And a ranch rider rode slow across the lane — Benn, watching

from distance.

No words spoken.

Just men standing where angels already stood.

The sect men, startled, backed away.

Their pride stung, their plans crumbling like sand under flood.

And in the Mercy house, Hannah slept unaware — her face soft, hands loose atop blankets, breathing peace for the first time in years.

Naomi checked her once more, tucking quilt edges.

Ellie whispered from doorway,

"The Lord does not slumber."

Maggie breathed,

"Nor does He abandon His daughters."

Outside, Hank lingered on the hill with horse reins in hand — not invited, not presumptuous — simply staying near like a silent watchman.

Marshal rode up beside him.

"You think they'll try again?"

Hank's jaw tightened.

"Not while I've breath and God has angels."

Marshal nodded.

"We stand then."

And the prairie, wind-hushed and moon-blessed, felt like holy ground — because righteousness watched and the Shepherd guarded His lamb.

Darkness failed that night.

Light did not boast.

It simply stayed.

Tomorrow would hold trial again.

But grace had declared territory.

And heaven whispered over the land,

The battle belongs to the Lord.
But the brave will stand beside Him.

CHAPTER NINETEEN — A FUTURE GIVEN, NOT TAKEN

Morning sunlight poured through lace curtains in soft ribbons, warming polished wood floors and touching the kitchen table where the Mercy Six sat with open Bibles and steaming tea. Hannah sat quietly at the end, hands folded, eyes lowered, unsure if she belonged at such a table of grace and strength.

She had washed and braided her hair herself today — and that small act of choosing steadiness made her feel like she had borrowed courage from heaven.

Ellie spoke first, gentle and firm as always,
"Hannah, we prayed about your future."

Hannah's breath caught.

Naomi smiled softly,
"A woman cannot heal only by hiding. She must also grow."

Ruth Ann slid a paper toward her — writing neat and elegant, a list of daily lessons and study plans.

Maggie placed a folded calico length on the table.
"For your school dress."

Josie set a fresh notebook in front of her.
"For your studies."

Lillian placed a ribbon of pale blue atop it,
"And your dignity."

Ellie asked, voice warm and serious,

"Hannah, would you like to attend our school?"

Hannah froze.

Her hands rose to her mouth.

Her eyes flooded, tears spilling like a dam finally giving way with no shame now, only release.

"You… you would allow me to learn?"

Naomi took her hand,
"We would be honored to teach you."

Hannah wept openly — years of held breath finally exhaled.
She whispered, voice trembling,
"They always said learning was rebellion."

Ellie touched her shoulder gently,
"Truth is not rebellion. Bondage fears education."

Hannah cried harder, but it was not broken sobbing — it was **rebirth.**

"Then yes," she whispered. "Please… yes… I want to learn."

Josie smiled through her own tears,
"Then today, rebirth begins."

Hannah bowed her head,
"Lord… You did not forget me."

And the women answered softly in unity,
"He never forgets His daughters."

The Pastor and Sheriff Arrive

Sheriff Porter and Pastor Hale arrived mid-morning, tipping hats as the door opened.

"We heard the Lord brought joy here," Pastor said kindly.

Ellie nodded,
"Hannah has chosen education."

The sheriff smiled broad,
"Then she already stronger than what she left."

Pastor Hale prayed with them softly,
"Lord, give this young woman a mind like Your wisdom and a heart like Your mercy. Let no chain return to her spirit."

Hannah whispered,
"Amen... amen..."

The sheriff set his hat firm in hand,
"Y'all stay alert. The enemy does not clap when captives walk free."

Ellie answered,
"We stand with God."

"And so, does the law," Sheriff Porter replied.

Revival in Town

That evening, Providence gathered mid-week at church, but routine service became something different — something holy.

Pastor Hale opened in simple prayer, yet tears fell across pews before the second verse of Amazing Grace finished.

Mrs. Kepper stood trembling,
"We seen wolves try to hide in flock's clothing. No more."

Voices murmured agreement.

The pastor read aloud,
"Stand firm therefore, in the liberty wherewith Christ hath made us free."

And suddenly — hands lifted, knees bent, hearts poured forth.
Not noisy chaos — gentle trembling, a wind of truth moving like fire in wheat.

Hannah wept quietly in the pew between Naomi and Lillian.
Country women who once only murmured greetings now came to her, one by one, touching her shoulders, whispering blessings,
"You safe now, honey."

"You're seen."

"You belong to God."

Scripture rolled like river water.

The Spirit was present.

The wolves' shadow trembled.

Rangers Witness Hannah's Healing

The next morning Hank came with Marshal and Boone to drop off a message from Carter about town watch shifts. They stood politely on the porch until Ellie called Hannah to the doorway.

Hannah appeared, still shy, but her eyes did not remain on the floor. She lifted them, just a little, and smiled faint and pure.

Hank's voice came quiet, almost reverent,
"You look... freer."

Hannah blushed,
"I am learning to stand."

Marshal nodded,
"God raises who men push down."

Boone touched his hat brim,
"And no man nor sect can undo God's hand."

Hannah clasped her shawl,
"I am going to school."

Hank's smile warmed like hearth fire,
"You will shine."

She nearly cried again at those simple words — not romantic flattery, but holy affirmation.

Naomi whispered behind her,
"God knit their meeting, not chance."

Lillian murmured back,
"And He writes the pace."

The men left with respectful bows, leaving gentleness in their wake.

— The Sect Pressures and Community Rises

By afternoon, word reached the Fellowship that Hannah would attend school under the Mercy Six.

Shock.
Then fury.
Then fear disguised as righteous outrage.

"She was ours."
"She disobeyed spiritual authority."
"She must be retrieved."

Their mothers sharpened whispers.
Daughters clenched fists in envy.
Men plotted in secrecy, pride wounded by heaven's rescue of one girl.

But Providence was no longer silent.
Women kept eyes open.
Men checked lanterns and rifles not to kill, but to protect.
Farmers offered escorts for the Mercy Six when they traveled.

A hedge of community had formed — not gossip, but guardianship.

Attempted Seizure Blocked by God and People

At dusk, as candles were being lit in the Mercy house and Naomi braided Hannah's hair with gentle hands, footsteps approached outside — hurried, heavy, intent.

Hank rose from the ranch bench half a mile away, sense tightening. He mounted quick and rode toward town, led by something deeper than instinct.

Two sect men moved toward the Mercy gate — shadows in tall grass.
But before they reached the fence:
The sheriff stepped from the dark.
The pastor from the path.

Mr. Hale with lantern.
Two farmers behind them.
And Hank on horseback sliding in from the road.

No confrontation.
No raised voices.

Just righteous men standing firm
and wickedness halted without touch.

Elder Bane hissed,
"She belongs with us!"

Sheriff Porter's voice was steel wrapped in mercy,
"She belongs where God placed her — under safety, not shame."

Pastor Hale added,
"And God does not return lambs to wolves."

The sect men retreated, not defeated by muscle, but by **light and community unity**.

Inside, Hannah had not seen — but she *felt* safety wrap her like a quilt.

She whispered,
"Lord… You truly fight for me."

Naomi kissed her brow,
"You are under His wing."

Ellie whispered from prayer chair,
"And wolves fail when heaven watches."

Outside, Hank exhaled deep, hands on his reins, whispering,
"Thank You, Lord."

And in the quiet Missouri night, angels stood guard unseen.

The battle was not finished,
but victory had already chosen sides.

CHAPTER TWENTY — LOVE THAT GREW LIKE MORNING LIGHT

Hannah woke before dawn, breath steady, not fearing footsteps nor commands, but listening to the quiet hum of a house at peace. Her lamp glowed softly. The quilt lay warm across her lap. She sat by the window and whispered,

"Lord, help me be new today."

The word "new" made her chest flutter. She never had permission to be anything before. Now she could choose steps, thoughts, dreams.

Downstairs, kettles clinked softly, and the smell of rising bread filled the rooms. Lillian tapped on her door.

"Ready for your first lesson, dear?"

Hannah nodded. Her heart fluttered — not like fear now, but like possibility.

She walked into the dining room and found a new ribbon beside her plate — pale rose, soft like early dawn.

"For your hair," Josie smiled.
"To remind you God gives beauty in place of ashes."

Naomi poured warm tea,
"And dignity in place of shame."

Hannah bowed her head, voice shaking,
"I don't know how to thank you."

Ellie answered tenderly,

"Live free. That will be thanks enough."

As they prayed over breakfast, a knock sounded — respectful, unhurried. Ruth Ann opened the door.

Hank stood there, hat in hand, morning sun painting his face with gold. He had bathed, trimmed his beard neat, and wore his cleanest shirt — not fancy, but earnest.

Hannah's heart caught like bird wings beating in her chest. Her fingers curled nervously around her cup.

"Mornin', ladies," Hank nodded. Then his gaze settled soft on Hannah.

"Mornin', Miss Hannah. You... look joyful today."

She blushed, the pink ribbon trembling slightly in her hair.
"I am learning joy."

Hank's eyes warmed in quiet amazement.
"And it suits you like spring suits fields."

Naomi hid a small smile behind her napkin.
Josie elbowed Maggie under the table softly.
Lillian nearly hummed with delight.

Ellie simply gave God a quiet nod of praise.

Hank cleared his throat — a little shy, a little bold.
"I brought a book. If you take to readin', I reckon it might help."

He held it out — **Pilgrim's Progress**, pages worn, corners softened by use.

He had chosen a book about leaving bondage to walk toward light.

Hannah's fingers brushed his as she reached for it — barely a feather touch — yet she felt warmth cascade through her whole frame like grace poured sudden and sweet.

"I... will treasure it," she whispered.

Hank swallowed, voice thick,
"And if ever you don't understand a part, ask me. I'll gladly—"

He stopped, words catching under humility.

Ellie finished for him gently,

"You will gladly walk beside her in learning."

Hank nodded, breath unsteady,
"Yes ma'am. If… if she allows."

Hannah held the book close to her chest like a promise.
"I would like that."

Silence came, but a peaceful one.
There was no hurry.
No fluster.
Just the soft beginning of something tender.

Hank shifted, suddenly shy,
"I'll be ridin' fence line today. I just… thought to bring it first."

Naomi answered,
"Love does not shout when budding. It whispers and lets God water."

Hank blushed a little.
"Then I reckon I'll whisper by bringin' breakfast biscuits next time instead of books."

The Mercy Six chuckled softly,
"Both are welcome," Maggie teased.

Hank tipped his hat, eyes meeting Hannah's one last time, warm as sunrise.
"God keep you today."

"And you," she whispered back.

He walked away slowly, each step steady, as though leaving something precious behind him — or perhaps carrying something sacred within him.

Hannah pressed her palm to her heart once the door closed.
"What is… this feeling?"

Ellie touched her shoulder, voice soft as prayer,
"Child, that is not fear. That is not duty. That is not a command."

Naomi finished softly,
"That is **being seen**."

Lillian added through gentle tears,

"And God does not send such eyes without purpose."

Hannah bowed her head and whispered,
"Lord... if this is love, make me worthy. Make me brave. Make me free enough to give love, not just receive it."

And heaven answered in the stillness,
You are already becoming.

Outside, Hank paused halfway down the lane and pressed a hand against his chest, as if steadying a new and holy weight.

He whispered,
"Lord... if this be Your plan, teach me to guard her heart like You do."

Wind brushed his face like God's approval.

Neither hurried.
Neither forced.

Love had risen gentle as dawn over a wounded land — slow, steady, ordained.

And all of Providence felt the shift.

Because real love — God-authored love — changes the air long before it changes the name.

CHAPTER TWENTY-ONE — THE SIEGE OF LIGHT

It happened in the late afternoon, right when supper biscuits came out golden and fragrant, and the Mercy Six were preparing tea. The sun dipped low, brushing the parlor curtains in honey light.

Then came shouting.

Hooves pounding.

Boots rushing the steps.

Doors slammed open.

Six masked sect men stormed the Mercy house — rifles raised, voices tight with desperate wickedness held behind false piety.

"Hands up. Come quietly."

Ellie lifted her chin, heart stilled in God.

"You dare threaten God's daughters in His own sunlight?"

A rifle cocked.

"Enough preaching. You come now."

Naomi whispered a quick prayer under breath.

"Lord, hedge Hannah's path."

Ruth Ann steadied her spine — not shaking, not flinching.

"Fear is not our master," she murmured.

Lillian looked at Maggie and Josie, courage knitted between them like thread in a strong quilt.

Maggie spoke softly,

"We go as lambs only because our Shepherd watches."

They did not scream.

They did not fight.

They surrendered with dignity — not to men, but to **God's timing**.

The sect men herded them out, tied wrists with rope not tightly — for even men of deception feared laying true harm on holy women. They placed them in covered wagons and rode hard toward their camp hidden in timber.

As they rode, Ellie whispered to Naomi,
"God is not late."

Naomi answered quietly,
"Nor will He abandon."

The wagon wheels rolled through dust like thunder held in wood — a storm of injustice permitted only until heaven decreed rescue.

Hannah Discovers the Abduction

Hannah returned from an afternoon lesson in Scripture memorization with Pastor Hale's wife and found the house empty — doors open, chairs tipped slightly, shawls fallen on the floor like petals after wind.

Her breath seized.

She dropped her books.

Her knees hit the floor.

"No," she whispered.

"No, Lord, no."

Sheriff Porter arrived moments later, pistol drawn, face pale beneath his hat. He read a pinned note on the door — hands shaking:

Return the girl.
Or the women never return.
We leave Missouri at once.

Our terms stand.

Hannah's heart shattered.

"I did this," she whispered. "They came for me."

Sheriff knelt beside her.
"Child, you are not to blame. Evil chooses evil — not you."

Hannah wiped tears with shaking hands.
"Where are the Rangers?"

The sheriff swallowed.
"I... I did not call them. Trying to avoid blood."

Hannah's voice rose, still fragile but burning truth,
"You avoided help. They are honorable men — not killers. They protect."

Sheriff closed his eyes.
"You right. But fear clouded judgment."

Hannah stood — small, trembling, but fierce in spirit.
"I cannot let sisters suffer. I will not be the reason silence kills courage."

She ran to the barn where the Ranger riders often passed through.
Horse hooves sounded in distance.

And Hannah prayed as she grabbed the bridle of a mare,
"Lord, send them. Send Your men."

Rangers Learn the Truth

Two days passed.
Word trickled slow and heavy like molasses grief.

Sheriff and mayor tried to manage quiet search crews, but rumors spread like prairie wind through wheat — whisper by whisper, breath by breath. The school site stood silent, tools untouched. Town women lit candles nightly. Prayer circles formed — solemn, whispered, tear-stained.

Children asked in trembling voices,
"Will the Mercy ladies come home?"

Pastor Hale gathered the town in church nightly, reading Psalm 27:

"The Lord is my light and my salvation;
whom shall I fear?"

Yet the pews trembled with worry.

On the end of the fourteenth day, near dusk, Hank rode into town for supplies and saw Hannah outside the sheriff's office, skirts dusty, hair undone, eyes red from weeping.

His heart seized.

"Hannah? What's wrong?"

She could not speak — she simply pressed the ransom note into his calloused hand.

Hank's expression changed — not rage, not panic — but **steel mercy**. A storm under quiet control. A fire that protects, not burns.

Marshal, Boone, Carter, Thomas, and Benn arrived moments later — sensing trouble in the wind. They read the message wordlessly.

Silence.

Boone clenched his jaw so hard a muscle jumped.
Thomas swore softly — not as sin, but as grief.
Carter removed his hat, bowing his head.
Benn stared toward the hills as if he could see evil breathing.

Marshal closed his eyes, inhaled deep, voice steady as mountain granite:
"We ride at dawn."

Sheriff tried to speak —
"But—"

Marshal turned slow, gaze steady, not hard, but **commanded by heaven**.

"You should've come sooner.
You feared violence.
But violence walks freer when righteous men stay home."

Sheriff lowered his eyes.
"You're right."

Marshal nodded once — not cruel, not triumphing — just truth.

Hank stepped toward Hannah, voice soft as fresh-fallen snow,
"No one take those women without meetin' God on the road first."

She trembled,
"I caused—"

Hank shook his head, gentle and firm,
"You caused nothing but heaven's movement."

Boone placed his hat on his chest,
"Six women of God carried off.
We ain't lettin' night hold them another hour longer than the Lord permits."

The sheriff whispered,
"I ride too."

Mayor nodded,
"And so do I. I won't hide from duty again."

Pastor Hale stepped forward, Bible in hand,
"Then I pray over every saddle and every soul that rides."

Children peeked from doorways.
Mothers clutched shawls to throats.
Men removed hats as if church service had begun.

Pastor Hale lifted his voice high, trembling but mighty:

"No weapon formed against them shall prosper."

The town echoed,
"Amen."

Hannah whispered,
"Bring them home."

Hank touched her hand — barely — but it steadied her like anchor tied to rock.

"With God's help," he murmured,

"we bring everyone."

And the prairie night held its breath as heaven gathered angels and men gathered courage.

This was not a battle of guns.
It was a stand of righteousness.

And righteousness does not hide from wolves.
It goes and brings lambs home.

CHAPTER TWENTY-TWO — WHEN HEAVEN DARKENS, FREEDOM RIDES

Dawn did not come gentle.

It came **restless**, as if the prairie itself refused to wake until justice stirred.

Wind rolled low across the wheat, not playful but warning. The horizon darkened where morning light should rise — clouds billowing charcoal and violet, swollen with power not yet unleashed. Horses in pasture lifted their heads, ears pricked, sensing command in the air.

Inside the Mercy house, Hannah stood at the window clutching the borrowed Bible Hank had given her. The sky churned like a great Hand stirring waters of heaven.

She whispered, voice trembling,
"Lord… is this Your sign?"

Thunder answered far away, deep and rolling — not violent, but **authoritative**, as though heaven cleared its throat before speaking.

Hannah pressed her palm to the glass.
"They are coming home today."

No fear.
Only certainty.

Downstairs, Naomi looked up from prayer on her knees.
"You feel it too."

Ellie rose slowly, eyes lifted,
"When the Lord sends clouds, He rides in deliverance."

Ruth Ann exhaled,
"The time of captivity ends."

Lillian gripped her apron,
"Heaven darkens when God stands between wolves and lambs."

Maggie stepped to the porch, skirts tugged by rising wind.
"Storm is a sword today."

Josie whispered,
"And mercy is its edge."

They bowed their heads together, speaking one chorus:

"Lord, deliver Your daughters."

The Sect Camp — Fear Trembles

In the woods where they held the Mercy Six, the air thickened.
Lanterns flickered though dawn should have brightened them.
Daughters of the sect glanced skyward nervously.

Charity whispered, voice cracking,
"This storm... it wasn't forecast."

Elder Bane snapped,
"God tests us. Hold firm."

But one young woman's voice trembled,
"What if... what if He judges instead?"

Lightning flickered distant — not jagged, but **straight**, like a
pillar of fire beyond tree line.

Thunder murmured again — voice of Judge, not merely weather.

Even the hardest men swallowed fear.

Hannah's absence had already unstitched their control; now the
sky itself pulled thread from their pride.

The Mercy Six in Captivity — Calm as Still Waters

While wind lifted canvas and rattled wagon ties, the Mercy Six sat in a circle, wrists still bound, but their spirits untied.

Ellie prayed aloud, voice unshaken,
"Lord, lead them like You led Israel by cloud."

Naomi whispered psalms,
"He is my refuge and fortress."

Ruth Ann prayed for the town,
"Let no innocent hand be harmed."

Maggie prayed for the Rangers,
"Give them eyes like flint and hearts like Christ."

Josie prayed for Hannah,
"Let no guilt touch her soul."

And Lillian did the boldest thing — she sang.

Soft. Steady.
A hymn that carried like warm oil over cold stone.

A mighty fortress is our God,
A bulwark never failing…

The stormwind heard.
Trees hushed.
Even the captors paused — unsettled by peace stronger than chains.

The Rangers — Heaven's Wind in Their Faces

At the ranch, the six men saddled horses in silence. No shouting. No bravado. Every movement deliberate — men preparing not for battle of flesh, but **rescue under God's banner.**

Marshal tightened his cinch and looked out over the darkening plains.
"It's time."

Boone lifted his face into the rising wind.
"He rides before us."

Carter murmured,
"Storm's on our side."

Thomas spit dust, jaw set.

"Storm's the Lord."

Benn checked his rifle — not to kill, but to defend if wolves chose death.

"No harm to them women, not one hair."

Hank tied his hat firm, eyes full of steady fire.
"We ride for freedom."

Sheriff Porter arrived, hat low, regret heavy.
"I should've called you sooner."

Marshal rested a hand on his shoulder, forgiveness offered.
"You called now. That's what matters."

Pastor Hale rode up last, Bible tied in saddlebag.
"No sword leaves scabbard unless the Lord commands. We go to retrieve, not to revenge."

Lightning flared again — not chaotic, but **vertical**, like heaven's spear touched earth.

"I believe the Lord commands," Boone whispered.

And they mounted as one.

Before they spurred horses, Pastor Hale lifted his voice through thunder:

"Though I walk through the valley of the shadow of death,
I will fear no evil:
for Thou art with me."

A strong wind swept the group — not cold, not harsh — **like invisible wings passing over them.**

They rode.

Not wild.

Not reckless.

Steady.

United.

Covered.

Heaven's cavalry leading earth's men.

The Town Watches

Women and children gathered at porches, hats pressed to hearts. Mothers lifted infants skyward as though asking God to witness their faith.

Old Mrs. Kepper whispered, "Watch the clouds."

Above the Ranger company, a line of light formed like silver through charcoal.

Mrs. Hale murmured,
"He goes with them."

The Storm Breaks

Wind roared as they entered the woods, pushing limbs aside as if clearing path. Horses did not spook. They moved sure-footed, guided by something more than reins.

Thunder cracked — not dangerous, but **declarative**.

Marshal shouted over wind,
"This storm ain't to stop us.
It's to shield us."

Hank's jaw clenched,
"And to remind wolves who they face."

The Sect Camp — Panic Rising

Rain had not yet fallen, but the forest dripped with tension. Canvas slapped. Horses stamped nervously. Sect men clutched rifles tighter, but hands shook.

One hissed,
"This storm follows them."

Another muttered,
"Maybe... maybe we erred."

Elder Bane snapped,
"Stand firm! We are chosen—"

Lightning exploded **behind** him, lighting the sky pure white.

Not hitting.
Warning.

He stumbled back, fear finally showing.

A sect woman whispered wearily,
"Heaven ain't with us."

The Mercy Six Stand as Deliverance Arrives

Ellie lifted her face to the storm sky above the tent.
"They are near."

Naomi felt wind move like breath of angels.
"Stand still and see the salvation of the Lord."

Maggie whispered to Josie,
"I hear hooves."

Josie nodded tears,
"And wings."

The first Ranger appeared through trees like a figure carved by the storm's hand, then another, and another, until six stood tall and solemn, drenched in holy purpose.

Marshal's voice boomed clear,
"We come under God's authority.
Release them."

Elder Bane raised a shaking pistol, but a bolt of lightning struck a tree beside him — not killing, but warning with terrifying accuracy.

The gun fell from his hand.

Horses reared.
Voices cried out.
Sect daughters clung to each other trembling.

The forest itself shouted,
Enough.

Marshal dismounted slowly, hands empty, palms visible.
Hank followed, eyes locked on the women, then searching quickly — finding Hannah safe behind town women who had

followed in prayer.

He exhaled relief so deep it shook him.

Boone cut ropes.
Carter lifted Maggie gently from wagon.
Thomas steadied Ruth Ann.
Benn shielded Ellie.
Marshal supported Naomi as she stepped down.

Not one woman panicked.
They came out upright, faces calm, like queens rescued by angels.

Lillian turned to the sect women who trembled, and said softly, "You do not have to live in chains."

Some wept.
Some looked away.
Some hearts cracked just enough for light to touch.

When Storm Becomes Blessing

As the Mercy Six crossed back into town, the sky broke open — not in rage, but relief.
Rain fell warm, washing dust and fear.

Thunder softened.
Lightning eased.
Heaven quieted its voice to peace.

Hannah ran to Hank — not into his arms, but to stand beside him, strength beside strength.

He whispered,
"You prayed us here."

She whispered back,
"And God answered."

Ellie lifted her eyes, rain on her lashes like anointing oil.
"The storm birthed freedom."

And Naomi declared,
"No captive returns to chains today.
Nor ever again."

CHAPTER TWENTY-THREE — THE BLOOD THAT SPEAKS

Rain washed the dust from Providence through the night, and by morning the world smelled new — like wet earth, pine, and promise. The Mercy Six slept safe in the sheriff's home, Hannah slept under watch in the pastor's spare room, and every house lamp glowed warm with prayers answered.

Dawn spread like mercy across the fields.

Hannah stepped onto the porch in borrowed shawl, dawn light touching her face like a Father's hand blessing His daughter. Her Bible was tucked against her heart. She whispered the scripture Ellie taught her:

"The blood of Jesus speaks better things."

Her voice trembled — not with fear, but awe.

"Better than fear.
Better than bondage.
Better than accusation.
Better than men's harsh words."

And as she said it, the wind shifted — gentle, warm, as if heaven nodded.

Pastor Hale walked up quietly, Bible in hand, face softened by tears he didn't wipe.

"You spoke truth, child."

Hannah pressed a hand to her heart.

"It wasn't me. It was Him."

The pastor nodded.

"There are moments in history when the Lord speaks louder than evil — and this week was one."

He opened his Bible to Hebrews and read aloud, voice trembling:

"...to the blood that speaketh better things than that of Abel."

Hannah whispered,
"The blood spoke for me."

"For all of us," the pastor replied softly.
"Where men demanded return to slavery, God answered with deliverance."

The Mercy Six Return to the Town Square

Later that morning the Mercy Six walked into town — heads high, pace slow, grace in every step. Townspeople lined streets not to cheer like spectacle, but to stand in reverence.

Ellie led, Naomi beside her, Ruth Ann behind, Maggie and Josie arm-in-arm, Lillian with her hand over her heart. Each looked like a pillar of holy strength — humbled but unbroken.

Ellie lifted her hand once, not to wave, but to bless.
"Peace to this town in Jesus' name."

A whisper swept through crowd:
"Amen... amen..."

Even the sheriff pressed a handkerchief to his eyes.

Righteous Response — Not Revenge

In the courthouse, the sect leaders stood trembling — not bound in rope, but trapped by truth. The sheriff stood firm. Pastor Hale beside him. The mayor behind. The Rangers leaned along the back wall silently — not vengeful, but **watchmen of righteousness.**

Hannah walked in last and stood behind the Mercy Six — not hiding, but covering them with the prayer in her spirit.

Sheriff Porter spoke, voice steady:

"You attempted harm. You tried to take what God shielded. Providence is not your field to plow with control."

Elder Bane opened his mouth, "We—"

Pastor lifted a hand, silencing him gently.
"We judge not today. Heaven already judged pride."

Scripture rolled from the pastor's lips:

"Vengeance is Mine, saith the Lord."

The room went still.

Sheriff nodded to the door.
"You may leave these lands.
You will not take daughters with you.
Those who wish freedom may stay."

Whispers spread.
Women in the sect looked up — eyes filling with hope.

Elder Bane's jaw clenched — control dying.

Naomi whispered,
"Let captives go free, Lord."

Hannah & Hank — The First Spoken Truth

Outside, Hank waited — hat in hand, breath held like a prayer.
Hannah approached, heart thudding gentle but certain.

"You came," she whispered.

He answered softly,
"Always would have."

"You saved them."

His voice broke,
"No. The Lord did. We only rode where He pointed."

Hannah looked down at her hands, once trembling in fear, now trembling with awakening love.

"Hank... I do not know how to love yet. I only learned to breathe."

He stepped closer — not touching, not crowding — reverence in his eyes.

"You breathe, and I'll wait."

Hannah's eyes filled.

"I'm learning freedom."

Hank's voice dropped to a vow, quiet as covenant:
"And when you ready, I'll teach you what gentle love feels like."

Not forced.
Not hurried.
Not demanded.

Invited.

Hannah whispered,
"The blood that speaks… brought you."

"And brought you here," Hank answered.

They stood there in stillness — two hearts rising from broken soil, watered by mercy, shielded by heaven.

No grand hand-holding.
No kiss.
Just a promise in the air — holy and safe.

The Mercy Six Speak a Blessing

Ellie stepped forward, voice clear:

"Today, we walk forward. The storm passed. The lambs rescued. The wolves sent away. Let this town be a sanctuary. Let this school be a light."

Naomi added,
"And let love grow slow and holy."

Ruth Ann smiled,
"As bread rises gentle, so shall futures."

Maggie whispered,
"Joy is returning to this town."

Josie lifted Hannah's hand,
"And God gives daughters families."

Lillian looked toward Hank and smiled,
"And safe men guard safe women."

The wind carried their blessing like incense.

And in that moment, all Providence knew...
God Himself had written this chapter.

The blood had spoken.
And freedom stood unashamed.

CHAPTER TWENTY-FOUR — BEAUTY REBUILT UPON RUINS

The boardinghouse stood quiet at first, dust resting thick on windowpanes, shutters tired from waiting. But when the Mercy Six returned with keys in hand, the old boards creaked as though recognizing footsteps it had prayed to hear again.

Ellie opened the door first, the hinges sighing like a home exhaling.

Naomi stepped in behind her, laying fingers on the banister.

Ruth Ann brushed a hand across the entry table.

Maggie opened windows wide.

Josie lifted curtains to let sunlight pour in.

Lillian knelt and touched the floor with a prayer,

"Lord, let this be a house of rising again."

It had not sold.

The lawyer confessed sheepishly when they returned to town office:

"I reckon God told me not to sell. I… felt the women would come back."

Ellie smiled.

"You listened better than many do."

Soon word spread across Providence —
the boardinghouse would reopen,
not as shelter only,

but as a new chapter for thirty young women stepping out of captivity.

The Sect Women Freed

At courthouse, Judge Holloway addressed the former sect daughters, faces pale but hopeful:

"You owe no allegiance to coercion. You are free under law and heaven. Stay here by choice, or leave by choice — but you belong to no man's rule but God's."

Every young woman chose freedom.

Only the sect leader's wife and the smallest children followed him out of town — fear, not loyalty.

The others remained, quivering like birds released from cages but unsure how to fly.

And Providence opened its arms.

Enrollment Begins — Blossoming Souls

The thirty young women entered the boardinghouse in groups of five, shy, unsure, clutching small bundles — a ribbon here, a threadbare shawl there, shoes needing polish and hearts needing gentleness.

Ellie greeted each:

"Welcome home."

Naomi measured them for dresses and work aprons.
Ruth Ann took names and recorded ages — sixteen to twenty-eight.
Josie assigned chores gently, like invitations not commands.
Maggie planned meals and schedules.
Lillian hugged the most trembling ones until tears softened into smiles.

They were:

- Soft-spoken but hungry to learn
- Modestly built but yearning to dress with dignity

- Curious, timid, shadows under eyes but **light waiting**
- Hair braided simple at first; soon ribbons and lace replaced plain pins
- Faces once pale with fear now warming with color
- Shoulders straightening little by little

Where there had been uniform drabness, individuality blossomed:

- pale lavender ribbons
- soft rose dresses
- gingham aprons
- lace collars
- handmade brooches
- simple but proud bonnets

Their eyes changed first — fear melting into spark.

School Opens — Subjects of Life & Grace

The school began with a bell rung by Ellie herself. Girls gathered in polished desks, books ready, hearts open.

Subjects:

- **Scripture & Character** (Ellie)
- **Literacy & Writing** (Naomi)
- **Arithmetic & Bookkeeping** (Ruth Ann)
- **Cooking, Baking & Nutrition** (Maggie)
- **Sewing, Laundry & Household Order** (Josie)
- **Etiquette, Social Grace & Public Speaking** (Lillian)

Additional studies developing:

- **Business for Women**
- **Land and Home Basics**
- **Mother craft (childcare education)**
- **Prayer & Devotional Study**
- **Community Leadership for Ladies**

Jobs created around the school:

- **Kitchen helpers**
- **Garden tenders**
- **Laundry assistants**
- **Class monitors**
- **Library aides (a shelf now, but growing!)**
- **Sewing room assistants**
- **Bakery girls learning yeast breads & pies**

Each student earned a **small wage** — dignity, not charity.

And the boardinghouse rang with life suddenly — tread of boots, swish of skirts, laughter hesitant and then sweet, hymn humming, chalk scratching, voices practicing polite introductions:

"My name is Clara. I enjoy baking bread rolls and reading Proverbs."

"My name is June. I came to learn and stand."

"My name is Lydia. I sew, and I wish to be joyful."

Their voices shook.

Then steadied.

Then lifted like morning choirs.

Rules of New Life

The Mercy Six set gentle terms:

- One year in school
- Chores as community learning, not servitude

- Scripture study each dawn
- Prayer circle nightly
- If courted, courtship must be respectful & allow schooling completion
- No girl forced to marry — ever again
- Strength encouraged, not silence trained

One girl wept as Ellie spoke the rule,
"No man may command your soul."

"I never knew I was allowed to choose my life," she whispered.

"Yes, child," Ellie murmured, smoothing her hair. "You always were."

Eligible Young Men Notice

The thirty new free women did not go unnoticed.

Providence was full of good men — farmers, merchants, smiths, millers' sons, the banker's nephew, two stable workers, a post assistant, three carpenters, a saddle maker's apprentice.

They suddenly found many reasons to walk past the school grounds:

- delivering lumber
- stopping for coffee
- bringing eggs for the kitchen
- asking the time (though they wore watches)

And every one stepped aside respectfully when any of the Mercy Six walked by — because they knew **what real womanhood looked like now.**

But **the six Rangers** were spoken for — though none yet dared speak it.

The whole town saw truth:

Those men wore a look when seeing the Mercy women —
not hunger, not conquest, but **calling.**

The girls whispered in giggles behind hymn sheets,
"The Rangers hearts are taken and don't know it."

Small Humorous Situations

- One girl dropped an entire tray of biscuits when a kind young farmer smiled at her.
- Another practiced curtseying so often she curtseyed to a goat.
- Maggie's bread class erupted in flour when a girl tried to whisk too fast.
- Lillian nearly cried laughing when three girls practiced polite greeting so stiff they toppled like fence boards.
- Josie found a girl ironing her apron twice — "Miss, I wanted my future husband to see a wrinkle-free soul."

Joy came slowly — like sap rising in spring.

The Boardinghouse as Haven

The old walls now rang with:

- Psalms
- lessons
- bread rising
- sewing needles tapping
- giggles
- pages turning
- new dreams taking breath

Candles glowed warm at night, and soft prayers rose like incense:

"Lord, shape us."
"Teach us joy."

"Heal our past."

"Prepare our homes."

Hannah looked over the dining hall full of women learning freedom and whispered,

"This is what heaven rebuilding looks like."

Lillian rested a gentle hand on her back, smiling with misty eyes, "And this is only the beginning."

CHAPTER TWENTY-FIVE — THE DAY HEAVEN WHISPERED "NOW"

It was a gentle October Sunday morning in the year of our Lord 1890, the kind of morning when the earth seems to hush and breathe in the presence of God. The maples around Providence burned with autumn glory, gold and scarlet leaves drifting like blessings through the still air. The sky, brushed clean by recent rain, shone clear as polished glass.

Inside the boardinghouse, thirty young women and the Mercy Six fluttered about like doves readying their wings. Ribbons were tied. Curls brushed. Bonnets pinned. Dresses smoothed and tightened at the waist. A few of the more nervous girls reapplied perfume three times, worried the scent of fresh biscuits would cling to their sleeves.

Lillian stood near the parlor table, hands on her hips, laughing softly as two girls tried to lace each other's boots while trembling with anticipation.

"My dears," she said, "there is no better way to enter church than with joy and haste mixed together. It shows expectancy."

Naomi finished braiding a young woman's hair, then tied a lavender ribbon at the end. "And expectancy," she added, "is the soil of answered prayer."

Ruth Ann checked the hymnbooks stacked for the wagon ride, her lips curved in a quiet smile. "I believe today shall be a blessed one."

Ellie looked over the group, her eyes shining with tender pride. "Every face I see holds light," she said. "The Lord has begun a new chapter in this town."

Josie straightened her bonnet, adjusted her gloves, and whispered to herself, "Lord, steady all hearts. Especially my own." She glanced toward the window where the Rangers' ranch lay beyond the hills and tried not to blush.

Maggie was last to tie her apron bow. "Well," she murmured, "if this isn't the prettiest flock of ladies Providence has ever seen."

Hannah came down the stairs holding her Bible to her chest, cheeks warm, new shoes polished, hair simply curled and tied with a soft ribbon Hank had shyly gifted her the day before. She looked like hope freshly stitched in lace.

"Are you nervous?" Lillian whispered as they climbed into wagons.

Hannah smiled shyly, smoothing her skirt. "Only the good kind," she said. "The kind that says something sacred is near."

And indeed, it was.

Across town, men were preparing too. Rangers polished boots they had once barely dusted. Hank combed his hair three times and nearly poked his own eye trying to knot his neck cloth properly. Boone accidentally put on his dress coat backward and only noticed when Thomas nearly choked laughing. Benn, usually stoic, practiced smiling in the mirror and frightened himself so badly he decided to let nature take its course. Marshal simply prayed, then straightened his collar and thanked the Lord for mercy greater than pride.

By half past nine, wagons rolled toward the white-steepled church. The bell tolled slow and solemn in the crisp morning, its echo gliding over fields and rooftops like invitation from heaven itself.

When the Mercy Six and the thirty newly freed young ladies entered the churchyard, eyes widened. Gentle murmurs rose. Smiles warmed. Handkerchiefs dabbed at sudden tears. These women, once fearful shadows, now moved like blossoms turned toward sunlight.

Then the Rangers arrived, dismounting with hats pressed to hearts, faces uncommon soft. Hank saw Hannah and froze as though time harmed to breathe. She cast her gaze down, then lifted it shyly again, and he felt God stitch the moment into his spirit like a promise.

"Morning, Miss Hannah," he said, voice nearly catching.

"Good morning, Hank," she whispered, the name sweet as prayer on her tongue.

Then they walked into church.

Usually, Sundays followed steady rhythm: hymns, prayers, scripture, benediction. But this day carried something electric, like the hush before a miracle.

The Reverend Hale stood at the pulpit with a thick packet of papers in his hands. His face wore a solemn, joyous expectancy. The sheriff sat in the front pew. The town lawyer sat beside him, nervously smoothing his hair, glancing now and then at a certain quiet, newly freed young woman who clutched her hymnbook so tightly the corners bent.

When the last hymn ended, Reverend Hale lifted his Bible and cleared his throat.

"Today," he began slowly, "will not be as other Sundays."

A soft ripple went through the church. Women paused mid-fan. Men straightened jackets. Babies even hushed as if heaven pinched silence across the room.

"I have prayed," he continued, voice trembling with holy weight, "and the Lord laid a thing in my spirit I did not expect. Yet I know it is Him. Some seasons call for waiting. Today calls for obedience."

He lifted the packet high enough that the morning light glinted off fresh ink.

"These," he said, "are marriage licenses."

Gasps fluttered like startled doves.

"Yes," the reverend said tenderly, "I asked the judge and the lawyer to prepare them. I believe the Lord is building households in this city. I believe God desires covenant here. And so, I ask, if any gentleman has been courting in his heart and desires the hand of a godly woman, and if any woman feels peace in that same direction, step forth now."

Silence.

Then breath.

Then movement.

Hank stood faster than his mind could catch him. Hannah nearly stood at the same moment. They looked at one another, startled by their own hearts, and the church gasped in delight.

At the same time, Marshal, Boone, Thomas, Benn, Carter, and Josie, Ellie, Naomi, Lillian, Ruth Ann, and Maggie all moved instinctively — then froze halfway down the aisle, realizing every other couple had done the same.

The church erupted into laughter, applause, tears, and pure holy awe.

The Rangers looked at the Mercy women, and the Mercy women looked back, all caught between humility and heaven's nudge.

Hank, cheeks burning, whispered, "Well I'll be, looks like the Lord done moved quicker than my wits."

Hannah whispered back, "And quicker than my courage."

Then thirty more young couples — from town and the freed girls — stood also. Young men who had prayed for wives. Young women who had dreamed of choice and gentle love. Hands found hands. Hearts steadied. Futures aligned by divine breath.

Chaos? Yes.

Holy chaos.

Sanctified joy.

Love multiplied like loaves in the Master's hands.

The sheriff stood suddenly, eyes full, and the young former sect woman beside him rose too, trembling and radiant.

The lawyer, red-eared but determined, rose with the quiet girl he had admired. She blushed to her ears but held his arm bravely.

In less than a minute, nearly **thirty couples** filled the front of the church.

Reverend Hale wiped tears from his eyes. "Well," he whispered, "blessed be the name of the Lord."

One by one the couples repeated vows — tender, earnest, some voices shaking, some laughing through tears. The church echoed:

"I do."

"I do."

"I do."

Thirty times heaven heard it.

Even the youngest children stared wide, sensing history birthing itself.

At the end, Reverend Hale lifted both hands and declared:

"What a surprise. What a day. And what a God!"

The congregation rose like a river of praise, voices thundered, hats waved, and the old church rafters nearly shook from hallelujahs.

Nobody planned it.

Nobody expected it.

But heaven had whispered **now**, and hearts obeyed.

Afterwards, outside in the autumn gold, laughter and hymn-hum poured like honey. The boardinghouse girls hugged the Mercy Six. The Rangers stood dazed and deeply touched. Hank and Hannah simply held hands quietly under the oak tree, as though afraid words would break the holiness around them.

Hannah whispered, barely breathing,

"What happens next?"

Hank bowed his head near hers. "Whatever God wills. Slow, gentle, right."

She smiled, the kind of smile that grows roots and never leaves.

And in the distance, leaves fell like confetti from heaven's own hand.

Providence, Missouri, was never the same again.

What a surprise.

What a day.

CHAPTER TWENTY-SIX — THE NIGHT JOY RAN THROUGH THE STREETS

Chaos did not walk to the boardinghouse.

It ran, laughing and breathless, skirts flying, boots pounding, voices lifted like sparrows at sunrise.

The women poured through the doors in a flutter of lace and ribbons and half-packed trunks, every room blooming with excitement. Bonnets were tossed on beds, hymnbooks tucked into small valises, and shoes matched in pairs with frantic triumph as if the whole world had turned into a bridal treasure hunt.

Ellie and Naomi tried to restore order, but laughter outran dignity and joy outran schedule, and soon even they were laughing so hard tears shone in the corners of their eyes.

"Think calmly," Ellie said, wiping her face and trying to sound stern.

"No one think calmly," Josie giggled, tying her bonnet strings crooked.

"It is a night for rejoicing."

Outside, husbands crowded the steps, cheering and waving hats, whistling soft respectful tunes, trying not to burst into the house like excited boys racing into supper. The ex-Rangers stood among them, boots polished, hair combed neat, grinning like men who had suddenly found heaven living next door.

Boone tried to stand tall and reserved but failed when Lillian peeked out the window; he nearly toppled backward off the steps.

Marshal stood steady, but his grin gave him away.

Thomas had his hat pressed so tight to his chest it may as well have been nailed there.

Benn shuffled his feet like a schoolboy afraid he might dream himself awake.

Carter looked up at the sky and whispered a quiet thank You, Lord.

And Hank, well, Hank kept staring at the boardinghouse door with a look so soft any angel passing by might have paused to marvel at it.

A few husbands began dancing, hands waving in joy, and others joined — boots thumping, dust rising, harmonicas appearing from nowhere as if joy had a music shelf in heaven and God Himself handed out instruments.

Inside, trunks slammed shut and dresses were smoothed with trembling hands and Hannah ran down the stairs holding her Bible as if it were a bouquet tied with grace instead of ribbon.

Naomi held up her hands like a captain trying to command a joyful flood.

"Ladies, do not forget your belongings."

"We won't," the women chanted gleefully as if belongings were the least important thing in the world.

"Do not forget your dignity," Ellie added, though she was smiling so wide it hardly sounded like a warning.

"Dignity?" Maggie laughed. "We will recover dignity on Monday. Tonight, we have matrimony, much matrimony."

"No dignity needed for joy," one girl sang, twirling herself right into a packing basket.

Laughter burst like firecrackers in spring.

And then, like a bell calling to the heart, someone whispered the Scripture the Reverend had prayed over the congregation that morning — Proverbs 8:12.

"I wisdom dwell with prudence, and find out knowledge of witty inventions."

"What a witty idea God gave the reverend," Lillian breathed, hand pressed to her heart.

"Yes," Ellie whispered, "witty, holy, and perfectly timed."

At last, after many forgotten shawls were remembered and three wrong bonnets were switched back to rightful owners, the Mercy Six and the thirty newly married brides stepped out into the golden evening light.

Cheering erupted.

Hats flew into the air.

Boots stamped.

The town square sang hallelujah without needing the word spoken.

And then it happened:

The husbands reached for their wives — kissing them gently, reverently, a hand offered, never taken — and each woman placed her hand into her husband's palm like a prayer being answered.

The six Rangers stood waiting in a neat row, hardly breathing.

Ellie stepped to Marshal.

Naomi to Benn.

Lillian to Boone.

Ruth Ann to Thomas.

Josie to Carter.

Maggie to... well, Maggie dove straight at Boone first then realized he had Lillian and turned red as a beet. Boone laughed so loud the chickens roosting across the square startled awake. Josie tugged Maggie's sleeve, whispering, "Wrong Ranger, darling."

The crowd roared with laughter.

But finally, Maggie found her Ranger — Carter, who had been holding his breath so long he nearly fainted with relief when she took his hand and kissed him.

And then came Hannah and Hank.

Hannah stepped slowly, eyes lowered in sweet humility and raised in holy courage. Hank held his hat in one hand and stretched the other toward her like a man handing his heart to God first.

Their fingers touched and they kissed each other.
A prayer passed between them without sound.
And the crowd quieted just to honor the tenderness of it.

"All right now," the sheriff cried, breaking the silence with watery eyes and booming voice,
"Let's take our wives home before they change their minds!"

Laughter rolled across the street like music.
Hank grinned so big even the oldest ladies fanned themselves to hide smiling.

And off they went — pairs and pairs of newlywed couples walking arm-in-arm and kissing as they walked toward lighted porches, warm hearths, and futures tied with heaven's ribbon.

Tomorrow they would return to talk sense, organize homes, set schedules, and reopen the school and boardinghouse. Work would resume Tuesday and life would settle — after the whirlwind of grace finished its dance.

But tonight...they would hold nothing back.

Tonight, Providence sang.
Feet stomped, fiddles played, babies giggled, lanterns glowed along fence rails, and love threaded every circle of laughter that rose with the autumn stars.

Women waved parasols.
Men stomped in rhythm.

A few folks shouted Amen at random moments simply because gratitude spilled faster than their hearts could hold it.

And through it all, unseen but certain, the Blood of Jesus covered the town — Hebrews 12:24 written over every home like divine ink:

The blood speaks better things.

Better than fear.
Better than past chains.
Better than schemes and shadows.
Better than loneliness.

It spoke covenant.
It spoke joy.
It spoke protection.
It spoke belonging.

Providence, Missouri, was alive with holy surprise.

And heaven smiled.

Epilogue — A Life God Built

One Year Later

Providence woke to church bells and spring sunlight, the fragrance of lilac bushes drifting across porches and the sound of babies cooing in cradles on freshly swept verandas. It was graduation day at the small academy once born inside a humble boardinghouse and watered with tears, Scripture, and courage.

Rows of benches filled the hill behind the school, ribbons tied to fence posts, families sitting proudly in Sunday best. The Reverend prayed over the morning, his voice warm as sunshine.

Lord, you brought once-frightened daughters into liberty. You turned mourning into dancing. You have not failed one promise. Continue to keep Your hand upon this town.

And a soft Amen rolled like a gentle tide.

The first graduating class stood in white dresses trimmed with lace, hair pinned with homemade flowers, eyes bright — proof that God rebuilds what fear tries to destroy. Among them stood many brides now mothers-to-be, hands resting lovingly over growing life beneath their gowns.

The Mercy Six sat in the front pew, radiant and laughing softly as they fanned themselves, each with a swelling belly of promise. Their Rangers sat proudly behind them, straight-backed and polite, shirts tucked proper, hair brushed neat — evidence that etiquette lessons, though born in chaos, had taken root.

When the final girl received her certificate, applause washed across the hill like a fresh river. Ellie whispered to Naomi, "We sowed in tears, but look at this harvest."

Naomi smiled with gentle awe. "And the Lord added increase."

After graduation, children played tag between oak trees, husbands escorted wives carefully down the hill, and the six couples stood together like pillars of blessing.

Hannah rested her head against Hank's arm, whispering, "The Lord has been kind to us."

"He surely has," Hank breathed, eyes tender as sunrise.

By late afternoon, the Mercy Six gathered privately outside the boardinghouse once more, now a training hall for young wives. They placed hands on the wooden rail and spoke blessings over those who would come after them.

Ellie said softly, "Mercy College asked us to return, but the Lord planted us here."

"And He sent reinforcements," Josie added, nodding at the new teachers from back east, bustling around campus dormitories.

"Now we walk our calling beside our husbands," Ruth Ann whispered.

"And raise our children in the fear and joy of the Lord," Maggie added.

"In community," Naomi murmured.

"In covenant," Lillian finished.

They lifted their heads, breathing peace like a hymn.

They were home. They were loved. They were fruitful.

And they had become the kind of women who changed a town simply by living in it.

Ten Years Later

A decade passed like gentle river water, carving beauty as it flowed. Providence had grown into a place of laughter, schooling, baking, babies on hips, and Scripture sung before dawn.

Children raced through the meadow behind the ranch house — nine boys and seven girls belonging to the Rangers and their beloved wives, rosy-cheeked and full of frontier spirit. Chickens clucked near garden beds as little ones tumbled across fresh-cut grass, braids swinging and tiny boots kicking up dust.

The ranch had expanded; fencing stretched farther, fields greener, barns fuller. The Mercy Six lived in six adjoining cottages the Rangers built by hand, connected by picket gates so the women could visit one another as easily as sisters crossing a shared hallway. Lamps glowed warmly in every window, and bread cooled on open sills like an invitation to heaven.

The farmers market bustled each Saturday, tables laden with frontier bread loaves, jars of wild honey, sacks of flour ground at the town mill, and steaming pies that could soften even the hardest traveler's heart. Children sold lemonade for pennies. Grandmothers haggled good-naturedly over potatoes. A fiddle player sat under a sycamore playing hymns between reels.

Under a white canopy, Ellie and Naomi taught girls how to knead dough with purpose, saying, "A loaf rises best in quiet faith — same as a marriage."

Lillian corrected posture and speech with a gentle tap and a kind smile.

Josie supervised sewing lessons — hems straight, aprons crisp, dignity always in style.

Ruth Ann kept tall ledgers of business accounts, teaching women how to prosper honestly.

Maggie broke warm biscuits and fed little ones while sharing Proverbs with their mothers.

And Hannah, with long flowing hair now long and unpinned soft as a hymn, tended the teaching garden near the school's edge, her children bringing her wildflowers between lessons. Hank could be seen nearby splitting wood, pausing often just to grin at his wife like a man forever grateful for mercy.

Every Sabbath evening, neighbors gathered for supper under lantern light, the table long as the Lord's blessing: bread steaming, stew fragrant, pies resting golden, voices humming hymns in low harmonies.

They prayed, they laughed, they lived gentle.
They spoke truth and kindness in equal measure.
They raised children in faith and love.
They honored God and one another.

The six Mercy women, who had once arrived dust-covered, unsure, and trusting only God, now stood like matriarch oaks — rooted, fruitful, delighted in the goodness of the Lord.

And folks who passed through Providence always left whispering,
"There is something holy in that town."

For the blood of Jesus had covered them.

Wisdom had guided them.
Love had grown them.
And God had kept them.

They were wives.
They were mothers.
They were teachers.
They were pioneers.
They were sisters.

They were living the scripture they once whispered in trembling faith:

He hath made everything beautiful in His t

Frontier Bread Recipes — The Mercy Six Collection

1. Ellie's Providence Prairie Loaf

A hearty farmhouse loaf, perfect for families and working ranch hands.

Ingredients
4 cups flour
1½ cups warm milk
2 teaspoons salt
2 tablespoons lard or butter
2 tablespoons sugar
2 teaspoons yeast

Instructions
Warm milk gently. Add yeast and sugar. Let bloom until foamy.
Stir in flour, salt, and softened butter.
Knead until smooth. Let rise twice.
Shape into round loaves.
Bake at 375°F for 35 minutes.

Brush warm top with butter and thank the Lord for daily bread.

Ellie's tip: "Bread rises like faith — patiently and in quiet."

2. Naomi's Faith-Lift Cornbread

Soft, comforting, and perfect with honey or stew.

Ingredients
2 cups cornmeal
1 cup flour
2 cups buttermilk
2 eggs
3 tablespoons melted butter
1 tablespoon molasses
1 teaspoon baking soda
Pinch of salt

Instructions
Mix dry ingredients. Beat eggs into buttermilk and butter.
Combine and pour into hot greased skillet.
Bake at 400°F until edges crisp and top golden.

Naomi's reminder: "Stir gently. Do not rush nourishment."

3. Lillian's Courtship Biscuits

Fluffy biscuits meant to win hearts and bless tables.

Ingredients
3 cups flour
2 tablespoons sugar
1 teaspoon salt
4 teaspoons baking powder
½ cup lard or butter
1½ cups buttermilk

Instructions

Mix dry ingredients. Cut in lard until crumbly.
Add buttermilk. Roll gently and cut.
Bake at 425°F for 12 minutes.

Serve with jam, honey, or preserved berries.

Lillian's note: "A gentle hand yields tender biscuits — and tender marriages."

4. Ruth Ann's Ledger Loaf (Economy Bread)

Simple, thrifty, filling — the homemaker's friend.

Ingredients
3 cups flour
1½ cups warm water
2 teaspoons yeast
1 teaspoon salt

Instructions
Mix water and yeast. Let sit.
Add flour and salt. Stir only until combined.
Let rise once. Bake at 400°F for 30–35 minutes.

Ruth Ann's wisdom: "You can feed a home well with little, if done wisely."

5. Josie's Sunday Sweet Roll Bread

For Sabbath mornings and celebration gatherings.

Ingredients
4 cups flour
1 cup warm milk
⅓ cup butter
⅓ cup sugar
2 eggs
2 teaspoons yeast
1 teaspoon salt

Cinnamon and sugar for filling

Instructions
Bloom yeast in warm milk with sugar.
Mix in butter and eggs.
Add flour and knead until soft.
Rise once. Roll thin. Spread butter, sprinkle cinnamon and sugar.
Roll up and slice. Bake 20 minutes at 375°F.

Glaze with icing of powdered sugar and cream.

Josie's heart: "Joy is a gift of the Lord — serve sweet things in honor of Him."

6. Maggie's Hearth & Honey Loaf

Soft, comforting, and fragrant.

Ingredients
3½ cups flour
1 cup warm water
½ cup warm milk
¼ cup honey
2 tablespoons oil
2 teaspoons yeast
1½ teaspoon salt

Instructions
Combine warm water, milk, honey, and yeast. Let bloom.
Add flour, oil, and salt. Knead.
Rise twice. Bake at 385°F for 32 minutes.

Brush with warm honey when finished.

Maggie's encouragement: "The Lord sweetens life in due time."

How to Start a Book Club

1. Pray for the right hearts and purpose
2. Choose a location (home, church, community center, porch)
3. Gather 4–10 women to start
4. Pick one book a month (faith-and-joy themes)
5. Set a meeting time once per week or bi-weekly
6. Open each meeting with prayer
7. Discuss key chapters, characters, lessons
8. Encourage every voice
9. Share snacks and testimony
10. Journal personal reflections
11. Close with group prayer and scripture reading
12. Rotate host or leader if desired

Helpful Scriptures
Proverbs 27:17
Hebrews 10:24–25
Colossians 3:16

How to Start a Farmers Market

1. Pray and plan your mission
2. Gather trusted vendors (bakers, farmers, crafters)
3. Choose location with parking and shade
4. Secure permission from town or church
5. Create vendor rules (honest goods, fair conduct)
6. Set weekly schedule
7. Prepare tables, tents, signs
8. Advertise through church and town notice boards
9. Create seasonal offerings — bread, produce, crafts
10. Encourage fellowship and community spirit
11. Teach younger women skills — grinding flour, kneading, sewing

Keys to Success
Consistency
Honesty
Clean presentation
Hospitality
Scriptural encouragement
Scripture for the gate:
Psalm 90:17
Deuteronomy 28:8

ADDITIONAL BOOKS BY AUTHOR:

https://www.amazon.com/author/
plussizewomensbooks

The Sinner's Prayer

Lord Jesus,
I believe You are the Son of God.
I believe You died for my sins and rose again.
Forgive me, cleanse me, and make me new.
I receive You as my Lord and Savior.
Take my life and lead me.
I belong to You now and forever.
Amen.

What to Do After the Prayer

1. Tell someone — confess salvation joyfully
2. Begin reading your Bible daily
3. Pray morning and night
4. Attend a Bible-teaching church
5. Be baptized as a public declaration
6. Join a women's group or Bible study
7. Serve your community with love
8. Remove old sinful habits as God strengthens you
9. Walk in forgiveness and peace

10. Write your testimony — someone needs to hear it

Remember
You are saved by grace
Loved forever
And born into God's family

Scriptures
John 3:16
Romans 10:9–10
Ephesians 2:8
2 Corinthians 5:17